# In The Money

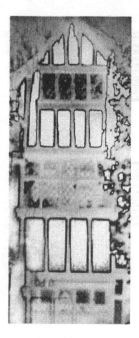

RED FOX DEFiniTiOnS

By the same author

GOING TO EGYPT

# In the Money

HELEN DUNMORE

RED FOX DEFINITIONS

A Red Fox Book

Published by Random House Children's Books
20 Vauxhall Bridge Road, London SW1V 2SA

A division of The Random House Group Ltd
London Melbourne Sydney Auckland
Johannesburg and agencies throughout the world

Copyright © Helen Dunmore 1993

1 3 5 7 9 10 8 6 4 2

First published in Great Britain by
Julia MacRae 1993

Red Fox edition 2001

Printed and bound in Great Britain by
Cox & Wyman Ltd, Reading, Berkshire

Papers used by The Random House Group Ltd are natural, recyclable products made from
wood grown in sustainable forests. The manufacturing processes conform to the environmental
regulations of the country of origin.

THE RANDOM HOUSE GROUP Limited Reg. No. 954009

ISBN 0 09 941187 3

www.randomhouse.co.uk

# Contents

*For Patrick*

# Chapter One

Dad sounds the horn loud and clear. The sound of a winner. We sweep round another tight bend and into a lane which is so narrow that the trees meet overhead. A green tunnel. We go faster and faster, rushing down the middle the way I do on the red flume at Water Wonder. *Experienced riders only, no children under ten, no stopping.* The fizz of bubbles in your ears and a booming scream from someone you never see. What if I get stuck? What if it's all a trick and the flume goes on and on, round and round for ever?

But everyone's laughing by the time they shoot over the lip of the flume and into the pool. Nobody ever admits they've been scared. Once you're out of that secret rushing tunnel, you have to pretend it was nothing.

"You going again?"

"Yeah!"

My head rolls against my padded headrest. There's no time left except *now*. The ride's never going to end. I'll never get back to safe ground again. That's what this journey feels like. We've only had this car for three weeks and Dad's still finding out what it can do.

We've got used to people turning round in the streets to look at us. Mum doesn't like it. That is, she likes the car, but I can tell she's not happy about us having a car like this, or about everybody looking. "What's this then?" she said when Dad brought it home the first time. "A new family car for the Tiernans? Why didn't you get a Porsche while you were at it? Then the neighbours could have had their eyes right out on stalks."

She made it sound as if she was joking, but she wasn't.

"Discreet luxury, that's what it's called," said Dad, and he made us all get in and smell the leather seats and the newness of it.

There's a groan from Shell in her corner. I knew those leather seats would finish her off. She's gone dirty white. With her head back like that in the headrest she looks as if she's sitting in the dentist's chair waiting to be drilled. Shell hates the dentist. He smiles at her all the time and talks in that reassuring voice dentists have, but it doesn't work with Shell. She sits there rigid and terrified. Luckily she's got good teeth.

"Paul," she moans, "I'm going to be sick."

"Dad, Shell's going to be sick."

We're all so used to Shell being car-sick that it only takes a few seconds for Dad to pull the car up, giving the braking system the best test it's had yet. He drags Shell out on my side because the bank's too steep on hers, and holds her head while she throws up into a clump of ferns. Shell is as neat as a cat when she's being sick.

The green silence of the tunnel rushes into the car. Mum and I don't say anything, but Mum sighs and shuts her eyes. We've been up since before five, and now it's 12.47 on my watch. My new watch. New car, new watch. New gold bracelet catching the sun on Mum's wrist. New everything. I think of our house, empty and echoing. We hardly took any of the furniture because Dad said it wasn't worth it. Some people came from Oxfam and took a load yesterday. Even the carpets. Mum scrubbed all the floorboards, so the house smelled of lemons. Dad didn't like her doing it though.

"What the hell are you doing that for, Angie?"

Mum straightened up, looking tired.

"I just thought I'd leave it nice," she said. "For the next people."

Dad flipped open the Yellow Pages and scored his finger down the rows and rows of CLEANING AND SERVICES.

"Then get on the phone," he said. "There's no need for you to do the dirty work."

Mum gave him a funny look, as if she was going to say something, but she didn't.

Shell and Dad walk back to the car. You'd never guess that Shell had been sick. She's giggling at something Dad's said. In a minute I know she'll start going on again about the new house and living in the country and her new school and the new friends she's going to make.

New. New. New. But you can't blame Shell, I suppose. She's only ten. And it's all coming true for her. A big house in the country. *A pony of your own, eh Shell? How about that?*

It's a new game where you get what you want as long as you don't ask questions. *Just like a fairy story.* Shell keeps saying that. But I don't like fairy stories. I never have. There's always a plot underneath about people getting punished, getting what they deserve.

The sun falls on the seats, bringing out the thick, creamy smell of leather. Shell and Dad get in and the door shuts with a rich *clunk*.

"Roll your window down, Paul," says Dad, and I

touch the electric button and watch the tinted glass disappear. Magic.

Dad starts the car and we glide forward, slowly at first, nosing our way down the lane like spies. Perhaps we are spies. I feel like one. I don't feel as if we belong in all this greenness and quietness. Spies crossing the border of a new country. Then the car swooshes faster, rocking round the corners. I don't feel too good. I'm not used to all this smoothness. But I'm never sick in cars, so I look out of the window and feel the warm air blowing over my face and wonder what's beyond the trees, and how far we've still got to go.

Dad starts singing:

> "We're in the money,
> we're in the money."

and when I look in the mirror I see his teeth and he's laughing, but I don't know if he's laughing at himself, or at the song, or if he's just laughing because he's got it all at last. He's got everything.

"Nothing like advertising it," says Mum.

Dad reaches out and puts one arm round her while he steers the car round terrifying corners with his other hand.

"Oh *Dad!*" says Shell. She hates Mum and Dad touching each other.

Shell, let me tell you, is very sharp. Now is now, as far as Shell's concerned.

*"Rich? Oh yes. Of course. That's nothing to get excited about. Isn't everybody rich?"*

She's been getting more and more like this ever since the money started, ever since money started pouring into our house like a river that had changed course. Soon Shell will have changed course completely too. I can just hear her when she goes to her *new school* with her *new friends*, talking about "*When we were in our London house*," and from the way she says it, everyone'll get the idea we lived in one of those posh squares you walk past on your way to Regent's Park, with private gardens and high walls to keep everybody else out. It's not that Shell will tell lies. But she won't mention the things which were really London for us: the smell of traffic, and Faisal's corner shop which is always open, and going to the Baths on Saturday mornings, and building a den in the park and getting shouted at by the park-keeper on his motorbike.

It's not that Shell's really a snob. She's just very adaptable. If a thing's true in her mind, then it's true. If we're in the money now, we've always been in the money. And we always will be. And Shell won't ask questions. Not the awkward ones. Just the ones that begin, "*Dad, d'you think I can have . . .*"

We shoot past a sign and Dad says, "Right, kids. Only two miles to go."

Mum and Dad have seen the house, of course, but Shell and I haven't. We asked if we could go with them last time, when they were planning the curtains and carpets, but Mum said no. I don't know why. Perhaps she thought I'd start boasting about it to my friends, but I wouldn't have. The stupid thing is, I don't even know the address. Everyone just kept talking about *our new house in the country*. I wanted to write down the address so I could give it to my friends, but though Mum kept saying, "Just a minute Paul, I'll get a bit of paper," she never gave it to me. And then it was all a rush, and we were going, and I forgot. But I'll write to Steve, as soon as I get there. Steve's my best friend. He lives three doors down, at number 35. He's always lived there.

Two miles is nothing, in a car like this. And now

we're so close, I want us to slow down. Suddenly, I don't want to get there. I'd rather the journey went on and on, just like this, with me thinking about *home* and home meaning London, not this new house which is going to become real in just a minute, in just a few seconds now. Once I've seen it, I shan't be able to pretend it's not real.

"Here we are," says Dad. "How do you like it?"

I stare across the big paved courtyard, past the row of four garages. I have seen houses like this before, on television, with carriages and horses drawn up by the door, and men going riding, and women with long dresses. And servants in caps and aprons. Gardeners bringing in loads of roses and black grapes.

On the television there'd be theme music, something rich and stately to go with the house.

"Load of rubbish," Mum would say, and flick it off with the remote-control.

But it's quiet here. The house is black-and-white. The white is peeling, as if it hasn't been painted for a long time. The black, the wood part, is grey in places, and it looks dusty. But the house is enormous. Row after row of windows with little diamond panes in each of them so that you can't really see in. It makes the house look secret. We get out of the car and stand there in the courtyard, looking at the house. There's a smell of dust, and a fruity smell, and the sun feels warm, as if it's trapped here with us. A bee drones past Shell and brushes the paving-stones, then veers up and away into the air. We watch it flying down the courtyard, past the house, through to the garden beyond. We can see the tops of wave after wave of trees. The house is at the top of a slope, and all the garden spreads out from it, downhill. Dad has told me. But you can't see much of the garden from here, and all we saw from the lane when we drove in was the high stone wall, hiding it.

Even Shell doesn't say anything. My heart beats hard. I keep expecting the door to open. I keep expecting someone to shout:

"Oi! You! What d'you want? What're *you* doing here?"

But there's no-one here. Just the big house in the sun. And us.

# Chapter Two

COLD HAVEN. That's the name of the house. The name of our new house. But you wouldn't know it, because it's not on the door, and there isn't a gate. Just the wide entrance for cars to sweep through into the courtyard. Anyway, it would look stupid if you had a little nameplate slapped on over that dark, heavy door. It's massive, like a dungeon door. The wood is dry and knotty and there are patterns in it which look like faces. The faces frown or snicker, but they don't smile. It's the kind of door prisoners could bang and bang on, all day and all through the night. Nobody would ever hear them. And we're so far from anywhere that no-one would come. But Dad has the keys, and they are just an ordinary mortice key and a Yale.

Cold Haven is the address, too. You don't need to write the name of the house, or the name of the street. There isn't a street, anyway, only the green tunnel lane that winds up to the house, and winds away again.

*COLD HAVEN*
*NEAR CALVERLEY*

Dad says the house isn't as old as I thought. I

thought it was hundreds and hundreds of years old, but it has only been built to make it look like that. I suppose that really it's a fake, in a way.

"It's late Victorian. That's about a hundred years ago. Built by a bloke who'd been in the Navy all his life. Then he came into the money and bought the land and had the house built. The lawyer told me. Like it, eh, Paul?"

I don't say anything. I nod. I count the windows along the upper floor. Attics? How many bedrooms? What's in them? *Then he came into the money.* Just like us. Is that why Dad and Mum chose the house?

Dad turns the mortice key, then the Yale at the top. The door slips open without a sound, as if it's just been oiled, or as if it's been waiting for us. Perhaps that makes it sound friendly, but it doesn't feel friendly.

Shell skids over the polished hall floor. The hall is huge, with a fireplace at one end, the kind you could roast a pig over, the way they used to at feasts. But then the house isn't that old, not nearly old enough for pig-feasts. I find myself wishing that it was. The house doesn't smell of food or people. It smells like an old book.

"Dad," says Shell, "where's all this furniture come from? Is it ours?"

"Yeah," says Dad. "I bought it at the auction. It came with the house. 'Course we'll get stuff of our own, too. But you won't find better quality than this."

He runs his hands down the long, long table. It is nearly the length of the hall. The wood is very dark, and it has a shine on it, a deep shine, different from the kind of shine you get on new wood, or on plastic. I touch it, too. It feels cold and smooth, but somehow alive. There are little hollows and rises which you can't see, but which move under your hands when you

15

stroke it. I bend down. There are knife-marks on the edge, deep ones, dark with age.

"Now that's really old," says Dad. "That's a monks' table. Think of those monks sitting round it at night, Ange, dreaming of a lovely woman like you."

"Someone's been polishing it," says Shell.

"Your mum fixed it last time we were down," says Dad. "A woman from the village is going to come in and clean."

"Wow!" says Shell. "*Servants!*"

"Don't be so silly," says Mum. "And mind you behave yourself, Shell. She won't want any of your nonsense."

"Where's the village?" I ask, thinking of shops, lights, fish-and chips, people . . .

"Couple of miles up the road," says Dad. "We went past the turning."

"There aren't any buses round here," says Mum. "Mrs Hannibal's coming on her moped."

"MRS HANNIBAL!" Shell shrieks.

"Yes. Her name is Mrs Hannibal. I thought I'd mention it now and let you get over it," says Mum.

Mrs Hannibal on a moped. I think about it. A huge grey woman, like an elephant, brimming over the seat. The moped puttering up the lane, straining itself under her weight.

I move away and look at the paintings on the walls. They're all paintings of people, but I don't think I'd like to meet any of them. A big man with gold braid all over him, red in the face, staring out over our heads. There's something about his face which makes me want to look away, even though his eyes are fixed high on the wall. The varnish is cracking like crazy-paving, so that he has brown veins in his cheeks as well as red ones. He looks as if he's been roasted over a fire. He looks angry. Next to him there's a picture of two children in green velvet suits, bored to death. Perhaps they had to sit still for hours and hours while the picture was painted, the girl holding a hoop, the boy holding a puppy in the crook of his arm. I move closer and peer into the picture. I think it's a spaniel pup. They're wriggly. It wouldn't have liked being held like that for long. On the children's left there is a thin woman who looks wrong in her fancy dress and her jewels. She might be their mother, I suppose, but she doesn't look like anyone's mother. The jewels just hang on her and look awkward and a bit sad. Mum would look much better in them.

"*A woman like Angie is made for diamonds.*"

Dad said that a couple of weeks ago, when he came home with a pair of diamond ear-rings in a blue velvet box, for Mum. He'd been drinking, but not much. Dad never does. He's careful that way. He once said to me, "Never trust a drinker. Loose mouths, the lot of them. They'll give away their own grandmothers."

When I grow up, I'll make sure I can carry my drink.

Mum put the ear-rings on, very cool, as if she wore diamonds every day, but later on I caught her looking in the mirror, turning her head so that they flashed in the light. She saw me looking, and she winked and laughed and the diamonds threw out red and blue sparks. That was a good day.

"We haven't seen outside yet," says Shell.

"There's plenty of it," says Dad. "Go on and have a look. Keep an eye on her, Paul, she might get lost. Look out for barbed wire. The place has gone a bit wild, but we'll soon knock it into shape."

"Mr Hannibal's coming to do the garden," says Mum.

"On *his* moped, I expect," whispers Shell as we go out of the door.

We walk round the side of the house, away from the

courtyard and the road and the garages. We go past a big, umbrella-shaped tree covered with dark red fruits which look like raspberries, only they are too dark. Some of them are turning black. This is where the fruity smell comes from. There are wasps everywhere on the ground, crawling and clambering over the fallen berries, then staggering away over the grass as if they're drunk. There are black spatters of juice where the berries have dropped on the paved slabs. Shell picks a couple off the tree, and gives me one. They are sharp and sweet at the same time. They taste crisp against my teeth and they make my tongue curl up. Just for a moment I wonder if they might be poisonous. I feel hot inside thinking of the one I've already swallowed, then I tell myself not to be so stupid. People wouldn't plant poisonous berries so close to the house. But I don't like the taste. I can see why they've just been left to drop on the ground.

Then we come round the corner, and there's a wide terrace of pale yellow stones stretching all the way along the front of the house, and round the sides. Moss and weeds sprout up between the stones. The terrace is big enough to ride a bike on, but you couldn't skateboard. It's too bumpy. At the front of the house the terrace is high above the garden, like the prow of a ship.

We go forward, and as we walk we see more and more of the garden, stretching away below us, sloping down to the woods which are so far away that their tops look feathery and soft. It's enormous. I can't believe it's all one garden. But there aren't any fences or hedges dividing one bit from another, so it must be. And besides, Dad said. Grass rolls down to a huge oak tree. It's dark down there, and shadowy. But out in the sun there are lawns, and bushes, and rough, wild parts where you could hide all day and nobody would see you. It would be brilliant for making camps. We could take food, and light a fire, and sleep out all night.

There are long stripy marks, wavery ones, all down the grass where it's been cut, and some big heaps of lawn cuttings which nobody's taken away yet. Then I see a machine like a park mowing-machine. It's been left there. I wonder who's been mowing, and where he's gone. There are paler bits in the grass, as if there used to be flower-beds but they are all overgrown now. Dad said the place had gone wild.

The garden is so still it looks as if it's holding its breath. Wild, and hot, and quiet. There are lots of bees burring in the ivy on the wall, and wood-pigeons calling out of the woods, but they only make it seem quieter. That hollow bare place down near the woods must have been a pond once, but it's dry now. It's all paved with stone, and empty. There's a statue in the middle: I can't see it properly from here but it looks like a man holding a fish. Really struggling with it. The fish is trying to get away. Its mouth is wide open. It might be a fountain. Maybe we could turn it on!

Lots of little bushes everywhere, clumps of them in the grass, then high banks of dark bushes leading down to the woods. There's an arch with a plant winding all over it, but it doesn't go anywhere. It leans to one side. Everything's tangly, and you can't see what's underneath.

Shell and I pick our way across the flower-bed at the front of the terrace and step up onto the greyish-yellow top of the terrace wall.

The drop's about fourteen feet. I grab the back of Shell's sweatshirt. I hadn't thought it was going to be so high. Not high for me, of course, but high for Shell.

"I'm all right," she says, leaning over so far that I

yank her back hard and she sways and for a moment I'm really frightened. Sometimes Shell's got no sense.

"Let's sit down," I say quickly.

We sit, dangling our legs over the wall. The stone feels warm through my jeans. I can smell honeysuckle nearby: a wave of it, then it goes.

Now I can see the way down from the terrace. There's a flight of stone steps leading from the front of the house. We didn't see them before because a tree which grows up from the garden has spread right over the top of the wall just there, hiding the steps. But you could still get down them. And there's another tree below us, reaching up. It's nearly got here. It looks like the sort of tree which ought to be clipped small and tight, but it's escaped. The leaves are thick and green and leathery, and we can't see much through them. There might be a nest. Shell kicks out, and the top of the tree shivers, and then it happens. A voice shouts:

"Oi! What yer doin' up there?"

It's a man. A man down in the flowerbed under the wall. He must have been there all the time, only when he was bent over we didn't notice him. He fitted in to the colours of the path and the plants. Now he's looking up at us. He's got a bunch of sharp sticks in his hand. His face is pointed and brown, covered with lines like crazy-paving, shadowed by a black hat which he's tipped right back on his head to look at us.

"We weren't doing any harm," Shell calls in a voice which I've heard before. Soft and neat. Her park-keeper voice. We always get Shell to talk when there's trouble.

"That's as mebbe," says the man. "But you're here where you din ought to be, aren't you? Where you from? I ent seen you before."

20

"We've only just come," says Shell. "We're going to live here."

"Oohh," says the man on a big breath. He gives us a long, slow look, up and down, every inch of us. Then he laughs. "Oohh. Right enough. You'll be the new littl'uns up at the house. Mrs Hannibal did tell me it was today you wus comin'."

And he bends back and begins to run the sticks into the soft chocolatey earth round some chrysanthemums. We can smell the earth from the top of the wall.

"Well, you be gettin' on with your games and I'll be gettin' on with my work," he says, "I've all the summer beddin' to clear."

"Goodbye, then," says Shell, swinging her legs round. "Goodbye Mr . . . "

"Hannibal," says the man. We can only see the top of his hat now, as he bends over the silver-leaved plants at the edge of the flower-bed.

"Glory to God, we've met Mr Hannibal," whispers Shell.

"Don't say *Glory to God*," I hiss at her. I know she's just imitating John-Jo's Mum, and John-Jo's my friend.

All those flowers belong to us. Everything belongs to us. Which way are we going to go? We skirt our way around the edge of the terrace, dodging the long, snappy branches of the rose-bushes. They are more like rose-trees. They haven't been cut back like park ones. They seem to be reaching out for us. More steps, wide shallow stone ones, blotched with yellow lichen as if no-one goes up and down them any more. The steps lead down to a wide gravel path which runs like a dry stream down to the old oak tree, and on past it between thick dark rhododendron bushes and out of sight. Or we could go the other way, down across the lawns, past the fountain, down to the woods and the field. Or we could cross along the bottom of the terrace, by the long flower-beds where Mr Hannibal's working. Or there's another path, way up there, turning the corner by something which looks like a big mass of bamboo, and is that a chimney sticking out above it . . . ?

For some reason neither of us wants to go past Mr Hannibal. But we can if we want. There's nothing, *nothing*, we can't do.

"Is all this ours, Paul?" Shell asks, in a little voice as if someone might be listening.

"Dunno. It looks like it," I say.

I make it sound as if I don't care. Shell doesn't know that my stomach has gone tight and I can hardly swallow. It feels like the first moment when you wake up on your birthday and everything's waiting to happen. All the wrapping-paper is still on the presents and the postman is just walking up to the front door with your cards. Nothing's touched or spoiled. I look as far as I can to the right, to the left. There aren't any fences. There's no barbed wire. No walls. Only lawns, and flower-beds, bushes, and then dark masses of trees.

"C'm on, Shell! Let's go!"

I race from a standing start on the crunchy grey gravel. It spurts up behind me, and I'm gone. I don't stop running. Shell's way behind, but I won't turn round, not even to see how far behind she is. Shell's fast, she'll catch up if she wants to. My feet thud on the newly-cut grass. My breath is hot in my chest. I catch my foot and nearly fall but I don't, and I'm off again, down the long wide slope of the garden, past trees and bushes and through the arch I've seen from the terrace, and on down and down to the woods.

I stop, and wait for Shell. I want to throw myself

down on the grass and thump it with my fists the way footballers do when they score. I want to climb the trees and light a bonfire and pitch a tent and play football and . . .

. . . and do everything they stop you doing in a park.

NO BALL-GAMES ALLOWED. NO CLIMBING.
KEEP OFF THE GRASS. BATHING PROHIBITED.
DO NOT PICK THE FLOWERS.

I roll over on my back and look up at the sky. It's pale blue, with very high, skinny clouds. Nothing is moving except that I feel the earth going round under me and the sky moving, too. The blue sky hides the stars, but I could see them if I had the right instruments or if I was down at the bottom of a well perhaps . . .

You can't really see the stars in London, because of the streetlights. Here, I'll be able to. Soon I'll know the names of all the stars.

I raise my head and look back. Shell has stopped. She's picking a bunch of flowers, round red and purple ones like big daisies. I watch as she arranges them with a frill of leaves and ties a thread of grass round them. Then she puts the flowers down, looks at me and grins and turns three perfect cartwheels, one after another without stopping. Shell is brilliant at gymnastics.

I get up and look for a stone. I pull my arm right back and throw it, as hard and as high as I can, into the woods. There's a crackle of leaves and twigs and a flurry and two birds come thrashing out of the trees, shrieking at each other, shrieking at me, shrieking at Shell.

"What did you do that for?" Shell asks.

23

I don't answer. There's the path ahead going down through the wood. Dark, and cool, and a bit secret. The kind of path you wouldn't want to go down at night. We try to walk quietly, but the wood signals ahead of us that we're coming. It's dry and dusty after the summer, and there's a strong smell like garlic. The bushes crackle and rustle. Shell and I walk close to each other. Everything is getting out of our way, hiding, lying low. And then coming out again, once we're gone. Even the wood-pigeons hold their songs back in their throats. The woods feel as if they are on tiptoe, leaning and pressing all around us. I look back.

"Shell, we can't even see the house! And we're still in our own garden!"

"You don't call it the garden. You call it the grounds," says Shell.

Trust Shell to know, the minute we get here. You don't say *garden*. You say *grounds*. It's lucky Shell's my sister. Otherwise, I might not like her at all.

# Chapter Three

"For heaven's sake, Paul, will you stop staring out of that window! You've been parked there since dinner-time!"

Mum whisks the cushions off the window-seat, gives them a sharp bang, and puts them back. Hands on hips, she looks straight at me till I'm forced to look back at her.

"Why don't you go and play on your computer?"

"I've been playing on it for hours. My eyes hurt. And you're always saying it's not good for me."

Mum frowns. "The trouble with you is, you've been on holiday too long. Well, I can't help that. I'm not having you sitting here staring at the rain."

"There's nothing else to do."

My breath has misted up four of the little diamond-shaped window-panes. It doesn't matter, because there's nothing to look at anyway. Outside the rain is streaming down. It's so heavy that there's a thick wet mist hiding the trees and the fields. The terrace is grey and shiny. The sky is so low it seems to blot out everything. I can't even think about seeing the stars on a day like this. There are no colours anywhere. If I was in London – at home – I wouldn't mind. I'd go round to Steve's, or we'd go up to the leisure centre, or the cinema, or . . . I don't want to think about it. It makes me feel hot and angry inside, as if I'm going to break something.

It doesn't ever look as wet as this in London. In London there are buses crashing past, and lights, and people splashing through puddles. Here, there's nothing. Even the builders aren't working today, because it's too wet. I like watching the builders. Dad's shown me the plans. We're going to have a gym in the house, and down by the silver birches they're excavating for a swimming-pool. A swimming-pool, just for us. Unbelievable. It's going to have a chute and a spring-board and a changing room. It's going to be kidney-shaped. I've seen pictures of it in the brochure, with bright blue water and sun and people swimming and having drinks.

But it's October now. We won't be able to use the pool till next year, even if it does ever get built. At the moment it's a mess of mud and yellowish puddles and rubble which the JCB keeps digging out. There must have been a building down there before, Pete says. They're going to have to excavate the foundations. The digging looks like a scar across the garden when you look down from the terrace.

"Ten-past-three," says Mum, looking at her watch. "I'll have to go and get Shell in a minute. Why don't you come? Get yourself out of the house for a bit?"

"I'm not going to Shell's school again. They all stare."

Shell has gone to school. There's a private convent school in Amberley, about five miles away. It's just for girls. They wear hats and blazers and they have their hair in plaits, or in bunches. I've been with Mum to fetch Shell a couple of times. And seriously, you would not *believe* the way they talk. The kids are as bad as the teachers.

"Oh Cordy, there's been an absolute *disaster*! Joker's gone lame. And *just* before the gymkhana!"

It kills Dad. It really creases him up. I wish I could make him laugh the way those girls do. One of the girls came to tea last week and he kept asking her lots of questions, just so she'd go on a bit more about her pony and ballet and Mummy and Daddy. Corinna, she was called.

But Shell seems to like it. She even seemed to like Corinna. When they'd gone up to Shell's bedroom, I could hear them both laughing and carrying on just like Shell used to with her friends back in London. As I said before, the thing about Shell is that she's adaptable. I don't suppose she's even noticed the difference in herself. But I have. Already, Shell doesn't talk quite like she did. If she went back to her old school now, they'd say she was putting it on. But I don't think she is. It's just that it's natural for Shell to be like the people she's with.

She's going riding already, at the stables up at Calverley. And she's getting a pony.

But I'm not going to school yet. According to Dad, there isn't a suitable school nearby, whatever that means. Not in Calverley, not in Amberley. But I suppose I'll have to go to school some time. After all, it's against the law not to.

Mum is still standing there, looking at me. Sharp, but not cross. Suddenly she says, "Why don't you put on your waterproofs and your boots and get some fresh air? Monsoon-proof, it said on the label. Anyway, a bit of rain's not going to hurt you. You could go and see if the pond's filling up."

"Oh Mum, it's boring!"

I don't mean that really. Boring isn't the right word for the way I feel. The hot feeling has come back worse than ever. Now I want to hurt something. Or someone.

"There's no-one to talk to here!" I burst out. "At our old house I had Steve and John-Jo and . . . "

I stop. I know by Mum's face I've said too much.

"'Course you miss your friends. It's only natural," she says, and then she sighs. I hate Mum sighing.

"Everything'll work out . . . " she says, but more as if she's talking to herself than to me. Then she seems to make a decision.

"Has your dad told you? He's found a school."

Why does Mum say that? She must know Dad hasn't told me anything.

"What? Where? When do I start?"

"Ooh, I never thought I'd hear you sound like that about school! You *must* be fed up."

"I'm not really. I just miss . . . you know. Home."

"You mustn't talk like that, Paulie," says Mum, but she says it quite gently. "This is home now."

"Where's the school?"

Mum picks up the curtain cord and plays with it, looking down, not at me any more.

"You know, Paul, me and your dad want you to have opportunities. The chance of a really good future. And now lots of things are possible, things we couldn't do before. Try to understand. The thing is, we think it would be best if you went to a boarding-school. Just as a weekly boarder, coming home at weekends. It's called a prep school. Then, in a year or so, when you're thirteen, you'll go on to one of the top schools. Public school. You're a clever boy, Paul. There'll be no stopping you then."

I can't think of anything to say. One look at Mum's face tells me that not only has this been decided, but that the place in a weekly boarding-school has already been booked and probably paid for. I wouldn't be surprised if they've brought my uniform too, and it's upstairs waiting for me to try it on.

28

"It's not going to happen straight away," says Mum quickly. "That's why we haven't sent you off at the same time as Shell. You see they do things at this school you haven't done. Latin. Advanced French. You'd be behind the others. So you're going to have someone coming to teach you till after Christmas, help you catch up."

"What, a teacher coming here? Just for me?"

"That's right. Only you don't call him a teacher. He's called a tutor."

Maybe Shell takes after Mum. Mum seems to know all the right words, too. A tutor.

"When's he coming?"

"Next week. He's ever so nice. Dad and I met him in London. He's just finished at one of those public schools I told you about. He's going to Oxford University next year, so he'll teach you till Christmas, then he's going abroad."

If he's just left school he can't be that old. Not too much like a teacher.

"What's he called?"

"Nick Howard. He wants you to call him Nick."

"Mum. All this. Was it your idea too, or just Dad's?"

Mum lets go of the curtain-cord, and sits down on the window seat. She crosses her legs, and kicks off one of her shoes. She yawns, and stretches. She looks tired. She's losing her tan from the week she and Dad had in Bermuda, just before we moved. Mum loved Bermuda. But Mum always looks good, even if she's tired. She had me when she was seventeen, so she's always been younger than other people's mothers.

"We both want the best for you," she says.

And there's no answer to that. I can tell she means it. And I'm not going to school till after Christmas. Lots of things could happen before that.

"Does it cost a lot?"

Mum laughs. "It's daylight robbery! But that's the way everything works. You'll find out when you're older. You get something back for it."

"What do you get back?"

"Oh, all sorts of stuff. Knowing people. The right people. Knowing how to get things done. It's like short-cuts. You know how you can drive around for hours if you don't know an area and you haven't got a street-map, not getting anywhere, wearing yourself out and wasting petrol. It's the same with your education. *You* could be working your guts out, driving round and round, while the kids at the best schools are nipping through the short-cuts. That's what these schools do. They give you the maps. And that's what people pay for."

I think of Steve and my other friends, at my old school. I think of the plaster coming off the classroom walls, and the way we have to photocopy everything because there are never enough textbooks.

"It doesn't seem fair," I say.

"No. It's all wrong really. But it's the way the world works, and not just here. It's the same everywhere. Trouble with you, Paul, you're not a quick learner, not like our Shell."

I know Mum doesn't mean school-work. I'm all right at that. She means the way Shell always knows how the world works, wherever she is.

I try again. "But you and Dad didn't go to schools like that. And you've done all right. I mean, look at this place!" I wave my arm out of the window, but all I'm pointing at is the thick white mist and rain.

Mum looks at me hard. "Paulie. You *know* what we want for you. Something different. Maybe a profession. Maybe you could be a doctor?" The way she says this, I know it's something she really wants. Something she's wanted for a long time.

"Mum. Why do you want me to be different from you and Dad?"

She looks at me sharply. Then she says. "Now come on, Paulie, be your age. I don't have to spell it out, do I?"

No, Mum. You don't have to spell it out. I should know better than to ask questions. I feel lonely inside, thinking of Dad, thinking of Mum. Thinking of all the changes and why they've happened.

Mum looks out of the window, at the streaming rain. Then she says, "Listen, Paulie. When you get to that school, if anyone asks you, say your father's in business. Just business. They won't ask any more."

"All right," I mutter. I don't like Mum talking about the school like that. It makes it seem too real.

"I'd better go. Shell'll be wondering where I am. So when you talk to Dad, don't pull that face, eh? Get him to tell you about the school. He went to a lot of trouble choosing it. I'm going to do some shopping after I pick up Shell. I'll be back by half-past-five."

And she's gone. The door slams, and the house is empty. Mrs Hannibal has gone home, and Mr Hannibal didn't come today, because of the rain. No builders. Dad's in London, not due back till late tonight. But I don't feel any more lonely now that Mum's gone than I did when she was here. It's so hard to talk to Mum and Dad now. It was never easy, but now it's like trying to touch them through a thick mist, like the mist outside our windows. And I'm afraid to get close. There are too many things in the way.

There are the men who come to the house. They're not friends. They come *on business*. They have big quiet cars that make a soft crunch on the gravel when Shell and I are in bed. There've always been men coming on business, but these are different. Sometimes I look down over the banisters. They have the sort of faces you can't remember, because you don't want to remember them. They're invisible men we're not supposed to notice or ask questions about. They don't have names either. And there are so many phone calls. Sometimes the phone rings and Dad picks it up and doesn't say anything. He just listens, then puts the phone down again. We don't ask, "*Who was that, Dad?*" any more.

Once Shell said, "I'm getting tired of all these wrong numbers, aren't you, Mum?" and Mum looked at her in a sort of grateful way and said how awful the phone service was these days. But I didn't say anything.

And Dad's out all the time. Or he's away night after night after night. *On business.*

But now the house is empty. That doesn't make it any more lonely. It makes it mine.

Attics. Cellars. Cupboards. Corridors. There's still a lot of this house I don't really know. I'm not bored now. I feel on edge, a bit excited, a bit afraid. Perhaps it's because of the new school. I cross the quiet, polished hall. I wish we had a dog, sleeping by the fireplace. I'd snap my fingers and he'd open his eyes and shake himself and bound over to me. A golden labrador. Hey! Maybe I *could* get a dog! After all Shell's getting a pony. A dog of my own. There's loads of room for it here. If I got a dog, I'd call him Goldie.

I take an apple from the fruit-bowl on the monks' table and bite into it. All around me, there are open doors. I'm going to explore.

# Chapter Four

This is one of the rooms we don't use. Dad thinks we might put a snooker table in here later on, and make it into a games room. But at the moment it's empty. There's a big stone sink in one corner, and a table with stains and knife-marks on it. The windows are high, and not very big. It looks as if whoever planned this room didn't think it mattered whether you could see out or not. Perhaps it was a room for people who weren't supposed to matter. You can see a grey slice of sky, and that's all. There's cream paint on the walls, but it's blistering and I can pull off long strips of it if I run my fingernail along the wall . . . like that. It doesn't matter. Nobody comes here. The floor is made of stone slabs, but they're not the same colour as the ones on the terrace. These are dark grey, and very smooth and cold. Anything you dropped would smash to pieces.

On the table there are a couple of glass jars and a heap of rosehips which have shrivelled up. Shell picked them, one day just after we moved here. I'd told her we could make itching powder out of the seeds. She's scraped quite a lot of the seeds out, but then she got tired of it. I was thinking that I could make this room into an invention room, and do experiments here.

There's a sink with water, and there's a gas tap where you could fix a bunsen burner. I've got a chemistry set.

It smells as if the windows haven't been opened for a long time. Dry, and still, and cold. The air's been used over and over again. It makes me think about the people who were here before us. The people who were here long ago, when the house was new and full of cooks and maids and bells ringing. There's still a bell in the corner of Mum and Dad's bedroom, but it doesn't ring anywhere. Shell tried it. She was hoping Mrs Hannibal would come puffing up the stairs.

Once the bells used to ring down here, Mum says. There's still a board with numbers on it. It shows which bell's been rung in which room, so you know where to go if you're a servant. One of the servants would drop what she was doing and scurry up all the stairs to ask what was wanted. The servant would have to put some coal on the fire, or fetch hot water in a big can like the ones up in the attics, or bring some more toast because the first lot wasn't crisp enough. Just think of it. Having to run and do exactly what someone else wanted, every time a bell rings.

I wouldn't do it. I just wouldn't. Even if they rang the bell all day long.

Why *did* they do it? Why didn't they just say: *Fetch it yourself. I'm not going to.*

Mum says they hardly got paid anything either, in those days. And they only had one Sunday afternoon off a month.

Mrs Hannibal's not a servant. She's only doing the cooking and cleaning to oblige, and because Hannibals have always come up to Cold Haven. That's what she says. And she gets lots of money: over the odds, Mum says, but she wouldn't come otherwise. Mrs Hannibal is saving for a holiday in Florida next year.

There are spider webs from corner to corner, with dead flies in them. Not fresh flies. Little shrivelled dry ones which wouldn't taste good to spiders. If you touched them the flies would explode into dust. I don't know what this room was used for.

There's a door in the corner. I opened it last time, and I was going to come back with a torch, but I forgot about it. It was sunny every day when we first moved in, and I was out all the time except for meals. In the woods, and down the field where they keep horses which are sick or have just foaled. And there are two young horses which haven't been ridden yet. The fields belong to us, but they're rented out to a farmer, and he told me about the horses. We can walk in the fields, though. The horses don't mind, but you have to be a bit careful of the young ones. They nip. They come up, and see if you've got anything to eat, so I keep windfalls from the orchard in my pocket. You have to hold your hand out flat, with the apple in the middle, and they pick it off. If you hold the apple out the normal way, they bite you by mistake.

I still haven't got a torch with me. I wonder if it's worth going back for one? Yes, it is. I dodge through the back kitchen and the main kitchen where the freezer's humming and there's a smell of roasting chicken. I don't know why I'm going up the stairs so quietly, almost on tiptoe. It doesn't feel quite safe to make a noise. One flight, then another. And the torch isn't here. But I'm sure I left it in my room! Who's taken it? No, here it is, under my swimming stuff. It's a good torch, waterproof and with a white, strong beam. I bought it a year ago. I had to save up for it for ages, out of my pocket money. The batteries are nearly new.

We don't really get pocket money now. There isn't much point in saving up for things if you know you can afford them anyway. Dad put £200 in an account for me when we moved here, so I'd have my own money for going out and buying computer games and stuff. I can use it whenever I want. I didn't tell Steve that when I wrote to him. It's all too different from the way things used to be. He'd think I was writing it to show off.

Back down the stairs, across the hall. This time I grab a banana. I'm starving. It must be the smell of roast chicken.

There's the same dry smell behind the door, and darkness. I sweep the torch round and there are steps going down, and round a turn. Then I see that there's a switch by my right hand, and I press it down. There's a glare of electric light from a bare bulb. It was more exciting in the darkness. Now it's only a flight of stairs going down to the cellars. But this is a different part of the cellars. The part I've been in before is where they used to store wine and potatoes and old machinery. Mangles, bits of tractors, a bike I thought we might mend but you can't get the parts.

This is different. It's warmer, and as I get down past the turn of the stairs, there's a smell that reminds me of something. A dry smell, the smell of something that used to be hot, but isn't hot any more.

Then I remember. At my school, my old school, we had a kiln for pottery. We used to have pottery club after school, and I used to help Mr Civitavese to take the pots out of the kiln after it was fired. When you opened the kiln door, there was the same smell. Dry and bricky. The smell of glazes and tiles.

This must be the old furnace-room. We don't use it any more, because we've got proper central heating now, with gas. But in the sitting-room and the hall and some of the other rooms, there are these vents like grids in the corners of the rooms, where the warm air used to blow up. Dad says it was how they used to have the central heating, up to a few years ago. The system was built with the house, a hundred years ago. Dad said it was quite advanced for its time.

The furnace is huge. Think of all the coal it must have swallowed. This place must have been a bit like the inside of a kiln, when it was burning. Or like one of the steelworks' furnace-rooms you see on TV, where the ore melts and goes white-hot. Up against the wall, there's a great pile of coke, and a shovel. The shovel's heavy. I pick it up, and swing it. Someone taller than me could shovel the coke straight from the heap into the furnace.

The furnace's door's standing open, just as it's been left. I wonder who left it like that. Who used to work here, when the furnace was burning? The shovel handle is cool in my hands. Someone's hands have made it smooth and dark, just here, where you grip it. Someone's sweat, from the heat. I dig the shovel into the heap of coke, and pull it out again, but most of the coke spills back onto the pile, and I drop it over the floor as I try to swing the shovel head into the furnace door. As I take out the shovel it catches on the door and there's a loud metal clang. It makes me jump. I put the shovel away quickly and neatly against the wall.

I thought I heard a door close. I listen the way you do when you wake at night and think there's someone in your room. I'm not used to the sounds of this house yet. The old wood in it creaks and ticks all night long.

There's something else, just behind and to the right of the furnace. In front of the wall, there's a second wall of bricks, painted white, almost up to my shoulders and about a metre across. The bricks are all laid right, the way brickies lay them, but they aren't fixed. They're only balanced. There isn't any cement between the bricks.

At first I just take one or two off the top layer. It's nice to feel the bricks heavy in my hands and swing them a little. Perhaps I'll use them for something. I don't know what. In our old house, Steve and I got the bricks from when our front wall collapsed, and we built a really good den in the back lane.

That's when I see it. The hole in the wall. A rough edge where I'd thought there'd be a solid wall, and black, empty air. I lean over the pile of bricks and put my hand in, and reach back as far as I can. Nothing. Just a hole, going back, with my hand waving in the emptiness. And a bit of breeze, coming from some-where under the house.

It takes longer than I think to pull the rest of the bricks away. I pile them to the side of the hole, so I can put them back, just as they were, in case anyone else comes down here. The hole doesn't go right down to the floor. It's square, and quite big. Big enough for me to crawl into.

But then, when I look closely at the edges of the hole, I can tell it's been made properly, like the rest of the house. It hasn't been finished off smoothly, but that's only because it's down here, where nobody bothers about what things look like, because the owners of the house wouldn't ever come down into this part. It's not secret. I expect they just piled those bricks up in front of it to make the room look neater or something. They weren't trying to hide the hole. It is edged all round with brick, red brick. A bit rough, but just a hole. It was stupid to get excited about it.

I could crawl in and have a look. I've got my torch. And there's plenty of room, so I wouldn't get stuck. I could easily back out again.

But I'm wearing a new tracksuit. It'll get ruined. Mum is always saying that clothes cost a fortune.

No, she isn't. She doesn't say it any more.

*We're in the money,*
*we're in the money . . .*

Right. We're in the money. If that means I've got to
move away from London, and our house and my school
and my friends and everything, then it means I can
ruin a tracksuit. They won't say anything.

It's easy to get in. I don't switch my torch on yet. Of
course there's the light coming in from behind me but
even allowing for that, the tunnel isn't as dark as I
thought it would be. It's not black. You can see a long
way down, and there's greyish light coming from the
end of the passage. Perhaps it leads outside. Hey! That
would be brilliant! A secret passage in and out of the
house. I could get in and out even when the doors were
locked. Even at night.

The bricks rasp through my tracksuit. I edge forward a couple of feet and decide not to crawl on my
hands and knees. It hurts. But I think there's enough
room for me to half stand, half crouch—a bit like an
ape-walk . . . Yes, that's better. And now I can hold
the torch properly. This place smells even more like
the inside of a kiln than the furnace-room did. It's dry
and dusty and I have to stop to cough. It really hurts
your stomach, coughing when you can't stand up
straight. I keep thinking I've gone a long way, but
then I look back and it's only a few metres, and I'm
nearly at the end of the passage already. The grey
light is coming in from the side somewhere, I can't see
quite where. Here's the corner . . . maybe if I switch
off my torch I'll see where the light's coming from . . .

A quick sound, like paper being scrumpled. Then
it's quiet. But not properly quiet. It's listening quiet.
The way I listen at night, when the cars come. But it's
not me listening. It's someone listening for me, lying

dead still, waiting. Someone who daren't even breathe for fear of me. Someone there, just round the corner.

# Chapter Five

 FREEZE.

Don't breathe.

Then back, back . . .

Back to the house. Shut my eyes. Don't ask who's there. I should never have been down there, looking.

No.

I'm here now.

It was only a little sound. No more than a bit of paper tearing.

A mouse. Or a bird that's fallen down the chimney. Nothing that'll hurt me.

I brace my legs because they're shaking. I hold up the torch like a weapon and I creep forward.

"*Doan 'it me. Doan 'it me.*"

It's like a rat's voice. Like the kind of voice a rat would have, thin and whiny.

The bobbling light and darkness settles into a pattern and I see her. She's backed up against the side of the passage, where it gets wider and there's a hollow she's fitted herself into. She presses herself back against the bricks. She's quite little. She's so skinny she must be hurting herself against the bricks. There's an awful smell. It's coming from her. There's sick coming up in my throat. I won't be sick here. I won't.

*"Doan 'ert me. Doan 'ert me."*

At first I don't know what she's saying. Then her language comes through to me as if I've tuned in to her, like tuning in to a channel on TV.

*"Don't hit me. Don't hurt me."*

My voice is angry and loud, much louder than hers: "What are you doing down here? This is *our* house! You're trepassing!"

The girl sits up a bit and stares at me. She looks better like that. Not sick and slumped any more, but like someone facing up for an argument in the playground.

She says in quite a different voice, nearly as loud as mine: "No it ent yer 'ouse! Iss th'Amiral's."

I haven't a clue what she's talking about, but at least she seems more like a real person now. Not like a rat. She's a real girl. But she still smells terrible. And I don't know if it's because I've only got a torch to look at her, but she looks a strange colour. Sort of grey. And there's a horrible sore round her mouth, with yellow stuff on it. It's crusty, and the yellow stuff oozes round the edge of the scab.

"What's your name?" I ask. There's lots of other things I want to ask, but I don't know how to start asking them.

"Sarah Louise," she says proudly.

"Oh."

"They doan give me me name 'ere. They gives me Annie."

"What d'you mean?"

She sighs as if I'm an idiot.

"They doan give me Sarah Louise cos it's too fancy, see. Servants doan 'ave fancy names."

I start coughing again. I can't help it, it's the dust and the dryness. And the smell. But I don't want her to guess that.

"You wanter watch that corf," says Sarah Louise.

I stop coughing and wipe my face on my sleeve. "It's the dust. It makes me cough." I don't want to say anything about the smell.

"Dust! They all say that," says Sarah Louise. "*I* know about *dust.*"

"What d'you mean?" I say again.

Sarah Louise looks round as if someone's listening. "C'n*sum*shun!" she hisses. "Lungs! I know! Me ma died've it! It makes yer corf jus like that. Corf n' corf n' yer corfin' yer lungs out."

She looks at me pityingly, as if I'm the one who's sick, not her. As if I'm the one to be sorry for. But I'm not.

"There's nothing the matter with me!" I say fiercely, "I haven't been to the doctor for years." It's a bit of an exaggeration, but it's more or less true. I don't get ill much, and Mum's never let me stay off school unless I'm ill enough to be in bed.

"I believe yer," says Sarah Louise in a sympathetic way. "Corsts too much, goin' fer th'doctor. I never seen a doctor."

She's sitting right up now, with her arms wrapped round her knees. Her eyes are bright. They're the only thing about her which are. Everything else is grey, even her hair. I've never seen anyone dressed in the kind of clothes Sarah Louise has got on. There are layers of them, but each layer is raggy so you can see the one underneath. Her feet stick out under the skirt, and they're bare. She's got a shawl wrapped round her shoulders. Even with all this stuff wrapped round her, you can still see how thin she is. Her elbows poke sharply out of the corners of the shawl.

"Why ent yer got proper clo'es?" asks Sarah Louise.

"What d'you mean?" Oh no! That's the third time I've said it! She really will think I'm an idiot. And why

43

does she keep getting things the wrong way round? My clothes are fine, and hers are horrible. She's the one who hasn't got proper clothes.

"This tracksuit's brand-new!"

Brand-new. And the label's on the outside so you can see where it came from. And guess how much it cost.

"C'm 'ere, then. Lessave a feel of it."

And she reaches out one of her skinny arms and pinches a bit of my tracksuit sleeve between her fingers. I feel her bony fingers rubbing the cloth of the tracksuit. Then she sticks her hand up the sleeve and feels the fleecy lining. I pull back. I don't want her hand reaching up my arm.

"Oooh! Iss ever s'warm, innit?"

Maybe I shouldn't've jumped back like that. She's so eager and friendly. She might guess that I don't want her to touch me.

"Are you cold?" I ask.

"*Are yew cold*?" she mimics me. "Sat 'ere wiv me bum on a brick for three days, is it likely?"

I feel hot and embarrassed. For the first time in my life I *know* that I'm rich, and stupid with it. I pull my tracksuit top over my head. "Here. You can have it."

But she shrinks back. "I'll get took up for thievin' it."

"No you won't. I'm *giving* it to you. Here. I've got lots more. I've got a cupboard full upstairs."

" 'Ave yer?" asks Sarah Louise wonderingly, as if she doesn't really believe me but she'd like to. She'd like to think of a world where people have lots of warm clothes and plenty to eat, but you can tell she's never lived in that world.

She takes the tracksuit top and tries to pull it on, but she gets it wrong and her arm comes out of the head-hole. I push it back and twist the top round till her head's in the right place. Somehow she gets the top on over the shawl. It looks a bit lumpy. She's much smaller than me. The top is still quite baggy on her, in spite of all the clothes she's wearing under it. But her face isn't young, even though she's small. It's an old face.

She grins at me. She doesn't say thank you, she just looks pleased with herself. She looks worse than ever now she's wearing normal clothes. Her thinness and dirtiness and greyness seemed to match her shawl, but they don't go with my brand-new tracksuit top.

She's dropped something while she was putting the tracksuit top on. I can't see what it is. A dark lump. I shine my torch down and pick it up. It's nothing. Just a filthy old crust of bread.

Sarah Louise flies at me. Her thin fingers grab mine, scratching as she fights to get the bread from me. They dig into me and her nails hurt me and I'm too surprised to fight back. I wouldn't anyway. Who wants her old bread? It's fallen on the floor and she scrabbles for it, scoops it up and backs against the wall again, her bread in her lap, her eyes on me. I back away myself. If I touch her, she'll spring at me again. She holds on to her bread as if it's her life.

"All right, all right! Keep your bread! I don't want it."

She doesn't believe me. Everybody wants her bread. I nearly got it, only she was too clever for me. She saw through my trick. I only gave her the tracksuit top so I could get hold of her bread.

"Hey, Sarah Louise," I say, not looking at her, making it seem as if it doesn't matter if she hears me or not, "I could get you some bread. Lots more bread. D'you want some?"

She doesn't answer, but I know she's heard. She's listening. Her body's tense, prickly with questions.

45

"We've got loads of bread upstairs. All sorts of stuff. Are you hungry?"

She still doesn't answer.

"All right. Be like that. I'm going."

A little creaky voice says: "Doan go up there. They'll catch yer."

And even though I know it's all rubbish, there's no *they*, just an empty house waiting for Mum and Shell to come home, for me to go upstairs and for Dad to get back from London, I feel cold.

"Who are *they*, Sarah Louise?"

"All of 'em. Mrs Cann'nball. She'll 'ave yer, f'yer thievin' up there. Mr Mord'n. All of 'em."

"There's only my mum and dad. And Shell. And . . . Mrs Hannibal. But she's gone home."

Mrs Hannibal. MRS CANNIBAL, that's what Shell and I call her, when no-one's around. MRS CANNONBALL?

"Gor, yer an innicen, ent yer? Yer doan know nothin'. Yer doan know th'Amiral? Doan know Mr Mord'n? Doan know *Mrs Perfeck*. Doan know *Mrs Cann'nball*. Gaan!" And she throws back her head and makes a scornful playground face at me which makes her look suddenly much younger.

"OK", I say. "You wait. You'll see. I'll be back with some bread in a minute."

But I hesitate. After all, it was nice of Sarah Louise to warn me about *them*. Even if they don't exist. She makes them sound as if they're real, but of course they can't be. They're names she's made up, that's all. Like Shell does. She's just making up a story.

Sarah Louise isn't like Shell, though. She's little and skinny and filthy, but her eyes are alive. They look at you. They look right into you. When you look at Sarah Louise's eyes, you don't think about the rest of her. And Sarah Louise's eyes ask questions. I think of Shell's eyes. Even when they're looking at you, there's something hidden. Secret. Was she always like that? When did it start? I can't remember.

"Yer want ter watch it," says Sarah Louise for the second time. "Mrs Cann'nball's queen in 'er kitchin. An she's hell on thievin'. She'll skewer yer like a woodcock if she ketches yer."

I don't want her to say any more. The idea of skewering is enough. Names are turning inside me like food when you're feeling sick. Maybe the air down here is bad. My heart thumps in thick heavy beats like feet running in dreams. I edge away, down the rough brick passage, catching my sleeve in one place, bumping my elbow on a brick which sticks out. Backing away.

Sarah Louise whispers after me. Her thin voice blows after me down the passage.

"Mind th'furniss! Mind th'furniss!"

# Chapter Six

There are so many different kinds of bread in the freezer. I don't know which to choose. Rye bread, pitta bread, currant bread, soda farls, white sliced, wholemeal, organic, soft-grain. All the bread you can eat, and then more. New kinds of bread you'll try out even if you aren't hungry. But Sarah Louise *is* hungry. I don't want to waste time waiting for the bread to thaw out.

In the bread-bin there's half a loaf of wholemeal, and a fresh crusty white loaf. I'll have that. Mum won't notice as long as I take another one out of the freezer.

I get out the knife and the breadboard and cut thick slices, butter them, and look around for a filling. Jam. No, peanut butter. It's full of protein and stuff. I smear on a thick layer of crunchy peanut butter, and put the sandwiches in a plastic bag so they won't get too dirty going down the passage. Then two apples, and a new packet of chocolate biscuits.

In less than five minutes, I'm back by the hole. I've got to hurry now. Mum and Shell can't be much longer.

This time I swing myself straight in, and down the passage. It seems shorter. Everything's easier, the second time you do it. There's the corner.

Sarah Louise is huddled up against the wall. She

looks cold and ill. Maybe it's because I've been up in the clean warm kitchen that the smell down here is worse than ever. She's slipped down the wall until she's half-sitting and half-lying. Is she asleep? I dump the packet of food on the ground and kneel down, shining the torch on her. She opens her eyes. She isn't wearing my tracksuit top any more. It's lying on the floor beside her.

"Oh. Yer 'ere agen. Yer bin ages. And yer clo'es ent proper clo'es. They doan keep yer warm."

" 'Course they do!" I say crossly. "What did you take the top off for?" I've just banged my elbow and it hurts. "It's brand-new and it's got a fleece lining."

"It makes me cold," says Sarah Louise stubbornly. "Why were yer so long?"

"I wasn't. I came as quick as I could. And I've brought you something to eat. Sandwiches."

Her eyes brighten. She moves a bit, but she doesn't sit up. "What yer got? Yer bin thievin'?"

"No. I told you. It's mine. It's our house."

Sarah Louise shakes her head as if she's tired, and takes hold of my wrist.

"Give it 'ere then. *If* yer got it."

I reach behind me for the food. I can't feel it, so I sweep wider, across the rough brick floor of the passage.

"Let go of me a minute, Sarah Louise. I must've put it down over there."

I shine the torch near to our feet, then wider, then round the whole passage, even up the walls and on the roof where I know there can't be anything. No food parcel. No sandwiches. No apples or chocolate biscuits. Nothing. Did I drop it? No. I remember putting it down, right here on the floor, a couple of minutes ago.

*What's going on?*

Rats. There could be rats.

Don't be so stupid. Rats couldn't whisk away a packet of food that size. Not without us seeing them. I shiver.

"Ent yer got it then?" Sarah Louise's voice, a bit mocking. Not disappointed. Not surprised. As if she hadn't expected anything, anyway. As if she never expects anything from anyone, ever.

"I had it here! I know I did!"

My voice comes out angry and frightened. But Sarah Louise isn't angry with me. She doesn't look as if she really remembers who I am. She looks too ill to get worked up about anything. I can't believe this is the same girl who sprang at me a few minutes ago, when she thought I'd taken her bread.

"Sarah Louise? Sarah Louise? Don't go to sleep! It's me, Paul. I've come back."

She opens her eyes again. "Yeah?"

"Are you ill? I mean—is there anything I can get you? Medicine or something?"

"Yeah. Get me some more a yer sanwiches." She shuts her eyes as if she's too tired to keep them open. She doesn't believe me. Maybe she doesn't even believe I'm real.

This time I don't back carefully out of the passage. I crouch and run. I stumble out of the hole, up the stairs, across the bare, empty invention room with the heap of rosehips on the table, through the main kitchen to the fridge. Milk. That's good for you when you're ill. What else? Hurry! She looks so awful.

And back down with the cold carton in my hand, and in through the hole, and along the tunnel, banging my elbows again and tearing the tracksuit at the knees. I'm panting as I reach out my hand with the carton of fresh milk, chill from the fridge, to Sarah Louise.

And the milk's gone. I close my hands, and there's

nothing there. My hand is still damp from the carton, and cold. I can't describe the feeling. It wasn't like dropping the milk, or someone taking it. The milk was just—*not there.*

Sarah Louise hasn't even opened her eyes. But she does when I shout out all the swear-words I know (and that's quite a lot), and kick hard against the brickwork until my foot hurts even through my trainers and I stop.

She smiles. She looks a bit better now. She takes her crust of grey bread out of her lap and begins to nibble on it, little nibbles which graze away bits of the bread. She chews and swallows carefully. Then she reaches behind her and takes out an old square-sided glass bottle, and drinks a bit of the cloudy liquid in it.

"Yer 'ere agen then," she says. "Gor, I wasn' feeling too good las' time y'were 'ere. I bin sick, see." She grins. "Doan go down th'passage! I bin sick down th'passage."

That must be why the smell was so awful. I think about being sick all alone down here, with no-one to hold your head or bring you a drink of water to wash your mouth out. No-one to tell you to get into bed and not worry about doing your homework, because you'll have to have tomorrow off school. Just Sarah Louise on her own in the greyish darkness.

But she looks a bit better now. Well, not better. But not so sick and faraway.

"Yer better take it," she says, pointing to the track-suit top. "Iss no good ter me. No more good'n yer sanwiches."

But she's not angry about it. In fact she looks pleased to see me. Glad to have some company. I think of the loneliness down here, and quickly stop thinking about it.

"Yer've got ter get up early in the mornin' ter get

past Mrs Cann'nball," says Sarah Louise, sympathetically. She's making excuses for me. She knows I wanted to thieve something for her, but it didn't work out. It's better if she thinks that. Less frightening than things just—disappearing.

"She's hot as hell on thievin' in 'er kitchen."

"Sarah Louise. Who's Mrs Cann'nball?"

"Why, doan yer know nothin'? It int 'er real name, a course. Iss jus what we call her. Us girls. But she's Mrs Hannibal an' doan forgit it. 'Er up above. The Holy Queen of Heav'n," says Sarah Louise, spitting out the Hs. "Mrs Kick-yer-arse Cann'nball."

Sarah Louise sounds tough, but her eyes are frightened. She keeps looking up as if she can hear a great voice roaring for her, a pair of flat black shoes tramping over the floor, a thick arm lifted to hit her . . .

*Doan 'it me. Doan 'ert me.*

Sarah Louise thought I was one of *them* the first time I came down. That's why she was frightened of me. She thought they had found out where she was, and were coming to get her.

"Does she—does she hit you?" I ask.

Sarah Louise leans towards me and pulls back her shawl. She rolls up her sleeve and turns her arm into the torchlight. There is a dark mass of bruises all over her arm. I can't see the colours of the bruises very well, but I can see that there are new bruises on top of old ones.

"She done that," says Sarah Louise. "An that's not all she done. She doan like me."

"Is that why you ran away?"

"No," says Sarah Louise. "I'm used ter beatin'. Dad beat us, when we was at home."

"Then why did you? What happened?"

Sarah Louise hesitates. This is different. She doesn't want to tell me.

She says hoarsely, "There's things goin' on. Things I know. *They* doan want me ter know. Things I seen."

"You can tell me. I won't tell anyone. I can keep secrets."

But she shakes her head and pinches her lips together, and I know she won't tell. She can't risk it.

I piece it together. She's seen something going on upstairs. Something *they* are trying to keep secret. But Sarah Louise knows, and *they* know that she knows. And she's frightened, and that's why she ran away and hid down here . . .

I think of the cars coming at night, and the men's voices, and the strangeness in our house. I think about the money and all the questions which have come with the money. Questions nobody answers. And suddenly I'm sure that's the sort of thing Sarah Louise is talking about. Not the same secrets exactly, but the same kind of secrets. Something hidden and frightening, something nobody's got to know about. Something it's dangerous to know too much about.

She's not frightened of beatings. So what does she think they're going to do to her?

"I'll tell yer this," Sarah Louise whispers. "Th'Amiral's in on it. The four of 'em's in tergether. Mrs Perfeck. Mr Mord'n. Mrs Cann'nball. An 'im. Now swear ter God yer'll say nothin'."

And I swear. I've got to. I can see the terror in Sarah Louise's face.

"I know how th'Amiral got the money ter build Cold Haven," she whispers.

"How?"

Sarah Louise says nothing. Her eyes shine, fixed on mine. She doesn't blink and I have to turn away first.

"Th'Amiral's money's bad money," she goes on. "Yer think all money's good, doancher? No. There's good money an' there's bad money. Yer doan know where it's come from."

"No," I whisper, but I do understand. I know what she's saying. And I know some of the ways the bad money comes.

And then I realise. I'm not thinking that Sarah Louise is making it up any more. I believe her. I don't know why I do, but somehow I know I've got to. She's not lying when she says that she's a servant in this house, working for the Admiral, working in the kitchens with Mrs Cannonball. And I'm telling the truth when I say that upstairs the house is empty, waiting for Mum and Dad and Shell, waiting for me.

But can two things be true at the same time? Perhaps they can. *At the same time* . . . Maybe that's the clue. Maybe they are both true, but . . . not at the same time. I feel as if I'm beginning to understand. It's like an itch inside my mind. But I can't think about it now. Not properly.

"Owd yer git past th'furniss?" asks Sarah Louise. "Dint yer git burnt?"

"It's not lit. The furnace is never lit now."

"GAAN!" she says, richly and scornfully. "Doan give me that! Th'furniss's allus lit. Never bin out since I bin 'ere. Never bin out, day or night."

"But it must go out in the summer."

"Howd yer git yer 'ot water? They shut off the 'eatin' ducks in summer. But it ent summer now."

"Well, it's only October. It's not really cold."

"October! Gor! Yer a real innicen, aren't yer? Doan yer remember Christmas? Dint yer 'ave Christmas?"

"Course we had Christmas! But that was ten months ago."

Sarah Louise just looks at me. "I'm not argewing with yer," she says. "But it's Feb'ry in my book."

I give up. Why argue? It's all mad. There's a girl

54

called Sarah Louise living under our house who's hiding from people who don't exist. She thinks it's the middle of winter, she's dressed in rags, and she's starving. And she's frightened.

But she's not frightened of me any more. I think she believes I'm hiding like her. She doesn't believe that it's our house, that we live here, that it's all safe. She thinks I'm hiding from all of *them*, too. Mrs Cann'n-ball. Mr Mord'n. Mrs Perfeck. Th'Amiral.

Who are *they*?

Sarah Louise isn't mad. I'm sure of it. You can tell by the way she looks at you. She's hiding because she's really afraid. She's so frightened she'd rather be here in the dark with hardly anything to eat than go back up into the house.

It's October. I know it. Can it be February as well? At the same time?

"Sarah Louise. Listen. I've got to go now. My mum'll be coming back, and she'll wonder where I am. And Shell. That's my sister. But I'll come back and see you, as soon as I can."

And I mean it. I want to see her, no matter how strange and confusing she is. She's different from everyone else in this house. She'll tell you things.

Sarah Louise gives me a bit of a smile. She pushes her hair back from her eyes. It's heavy, and dirty, and it doesn't look as if it ever gets washed or brushed or cut. It's hard to tell what colour it is, because there's a lot of brick-dust on it. There are fresh smears of dirt on top of the grey, worn-in dirt on her face. Maybe she's been crying. I wish I had something to give her. Something that wouldn't disappear before she gets it, the way the food and the milk did. Something which would keep her company.

I have a great idea. I take off my watch and pass it to her.

"Here. You can have this. Then you'll know what time it is." It's a digital watch. I press the button to show the time. "Look. 17.04. It's got the date, too. See. 23.10.92. October the 23rd, 1992. You see. I was right."

"Yer barmy," says Sarah Louise. "It ent nineteen-ninety-two. *Eighteen*-ninety-two, yer mean. This ent a pocket watch. Where'd yer nick it?"

I feel cold all over. I drop the watch in her lap, and say in a voice which comes out much too loud, almost a shout, "I've got to go! I've got to get back!"

"Awwright, yer got ter go. Who's stoppin' yer?"

She picks up her bread again and starts gnawing it, like Shell's hamster. I look back as I go round the corner and she's still got the bread up to her mouth. She's looking at the roof of the passage, as if she can hear sounds coming through it. The sounds of feet and voices. The roar of a kitchen. The smells of food cooking, a hundred years ago.

# Chapter Seven

But I haven't been back.

It's six days now since I saw Sarah Louise, but I haven't been back.

It sounds awful. That's because it *is* awful. I thought I'd go back as soon as I could, as soon as I had a chance to slip through the scullery and down the cellar stairs and into the passage. I wasn't going to leave Sarah Louise alone.

There's a voice inside me which keeps asking questions:

*What's the matter with you? There's a girl hiding under your house, and she's only got a crust of bread to eat, and she's ill, and, and, and ...*

*And you've just left her there?*

*Without trying to help her?*

*And you don't want to go back?*

*Because you're frightened?*

When I think about Sarah Louise my heart beats hard, the way it does at school when someone's about to get into serious trouble, and you don't know who it is, but it might be you. That moment when the teacher says nothing but looks at the class, at all the kids, one after another. That moment when even the kids who haven't done anything go red and shift in their seats and start scrabbling through their minds to see if there's anything at all which might make the teacher's eyes stop on them.

*Who's responsible for this? Was it one of you? Was it you?*

I'm frightened in case she's still there, all sick and smelly and bony, and I'm frightened in case she's not there. Or in case there's just a huddle of grey rags which doesn't move any more.

Yes, I'm afraid of all that. But those aren't the real reasons I don't want to go back and see Sarah Louise. There's something else. It's the way she makes me ask questions. I can't get out of my mind what she said about *good money* and *bad money*. And I can't stop thinking of our money. I've got the feeling that Sarah Louise would know straightaway what sort of money ours was. She's got those eyes that look right into you. She's not playing the hiding game, even though she's crouched under the house scared to death.

Nick came a few days ago. Nick is my new tutor. He's got his own car, an old MG, a dark green one. He swung it round into our courtyard, going much too fast. He braked hard and then just sat there, smiling, while Shell and I came up to say hello. We felt embarrassed. He looked so much at home that it didn't feel right for us to be welcoming him. And Mum wasn't there. She'd had to go up to London again, with Dad. Business.

Nick's got the longest legs I've ever seen on a human being. They are thin, too, and they don't look as if they're put together right at the knees and the ankles. All of a sudden the joints might go the wrong way and he'd fold up on the floor like a pair of compasses. You should have seen him climbing out of the car. First a bony knee went up like the kind of mountain peak little kids draw. Then his foot felt its way down the outside of the car, and a long prickly-tweed spider's leg came after it. Then another. I couldn't help thinking there might be more coming. Six legs. Eight legs. Then he scissored over to where we were standing.

"Hi, you two," he said in a sort of lazy, blurred voice as if he couldn't be bothered to say the words separately, "Now let me guess. Which one is Paul?"

Pathetic. Just because Shell was wearing her old jeans and had her hair tucked up in her baseball cap. Anyone could tell she was a girl. And I wasn't exactly wearing a skirt.

"OK if I leave her here?" he asked. He meant the car. We just nodded. He started dragging some old bashed-about cases which he'd wedged in behind the driving seat. Neither of us offered to help.

"Well, I was wrong," he said. "I thought you'd be all cheery chatter, coming from London."

"Like Eastenders, you mean," said Shell. She didn't put any expression into it, but he gave her a sharp look all the same as he picked up his cases.

Mrs Hannibal was in the kitchen, rolling out pastry for an apple pie.

"Morning Mr Nicholas," she said, not looking at him, but with a little smile pouching her mouth. He came up behind her and put down one of the cases so he could take a frill of pastry off the table.

"I've got better'n that if you're hungry," she said, rolling out the pastry with long firm sweeps, and then giving him just a bit of her smile. "Bakewell tart in the tin."

"Marvellous, Mrs H, you're a wonder," said Nick, and reached up a long arm to the shelf and took down the cake-tin. He picked the fattest, most glistening square of Bakewell tart from the top layer. I'm sure if we hadn't been looking he'd have dug down underneath for an even bigger piece.

He made lots more 'mm, marvellous,' noises while he was eating it. Then he started asking about Mr Hannibal and how all the Hannibal family were. Mrs Hannibal told him that her Evie had got a job in McDonalds in Calverley which was a terrible waste because she was such a bright girl and she'd done really well at school . . . and so on and so on with Nick looking at her as if he was watching a brilliant programme on TV and he couldn't wait for the next episode.

We hadn't even heard of Evie, or any of the other people they both knew. Nick perched on the table she was working on. He would have swung his legs, only they were too long. It was just as if we weren't there at all. As if we didn't even exist. It gave me the strangest feeling. I felt as if I was a ghost, watching people in the house I used to live in when I was alive. Mrs Hannibal went on smiling and talking and rolling pastry and fitting it round a yellow dish and cutting off the bits, and Nick popped them into his mouth even though he had his second slice of Bakewell tart in his hand. It was as if he lived here, and he'd just come home. He knew it, too. He was showing off to us. I was glad Mum wasn't there.

"You're in the yellow room, Mr Nick," said Mrs Hannibal. "I'd take you up, but I'm all flour. One of the children'll show you."

"It's OK, Mrs H. I know the way."

"Course you do. I was forgettin' . . . "

"Like the back of my hand," said Nick.

And he did. He swung straight up the stairs, round to the second flight and onto our floor.

"D'you know our house, then?" I asked.

"Oh yes, everyone round here knows Cold Haven," said Nick. "They used to have the most marvellous parties here when I was a kid. Children's parties."

"Who were the children?"

"Catherine . . . Piers . . . Nicolette . . . Claudia . . . "
he said, counting them off as if they were names he'd
just made up that moment.

"But who were they?"

"Questions, questions! They were the children of the
house. But the money ran out. They couldn't keep
the place going any longer." His voice was light but
regretful. Of course it would have been so much better
if they had been able to stay. Then there would have
been no need for people like us to buy Cold Haven. We
were at the door of his room. Yellow light shone off
the walls.

"Good. You've kept it yellow," said Nick. "This has
always been the yellow room. Thought you might have
changed it."

"Did you come here a lot, then?"

"Oh, you know. The usual. Everybody knows everybody in the country. Piers and I used to shoot squirrels.
But then the money ran out."

How strange. If they'd stayed, we wouldn't be here
now. I wouldn't be talking to Nick.

"The old Admiral's money fi-na-lly ran *out*," said
Nick.

The word tore through me like an electric current.
The old Admiral. I stepped forward. "Nick . . . "

But Nick had heaved his cases through the doorway.
He stepped into the yellow room and shut the door on
me with a smooth, polite click.

The yellow room is opposite my room and Shell's
room, with the stairwell between us. A wide gallery
runs all around the stairwell, and our rooms open off
it. You look down two floors into the hall, and the
refectory table shines up at you. Nick shares our bathroom, too. That's another thing about this house.
There's a kids' bathroom, which is all in yellow, then

there's a bathroom just for Mum and Dad, which is sea-green, and a white bathroom for visitors. Nick's not a visitor, then. We pay him, but you wouldn't guess that because Nick doesn't act at all like someone who's being paid to do a job. Nick's family only lives about ten miles away, but he's going to stay here during the week. The first evening, when Mum came back, I heard Nick saying to her, "It's an absolute morgue at home during term-time."

This is how Nick talks all the time. And all the time in that see-saw slurry voice. I don't like listening to him.

He eats more than anyone I've ever seen, but quickly and neatly so you don't think he's greedy. Mrs Hannibal's cooking most of our meals now, because Mum has to keep going up to London, like Dad. On business. Mum and Dad don't eat supper with us any more.

Mrs Hannibal likes Nick much more than she likes us. You can tell. He usually calls her Mrs H, and he's always making her laugh. He makes stupid jokes about elephants, which aren't funny at all and which I'm sure she's heard a million times, but she still laughs. Nick's only been here a few days, but he's already got her making the kind of food he likes. She's going to make him something called 'spotted dick' tonight, because he used to have it at school. I didn't know what it was, nor did Shell, but it's a sort of pudding with currants in it. Nick often talks about his old school. The more I hear about it, the less I want to think about going to anywhere like the school Nick's been to.

Mrs Hannibal. Yesterday I called her Mrs Cann'n-ball by mistake. I was thinking of Sarah Louise. She was cross, but she covered it up. For a minute I thought of what Sarah Louise called her: *Mrs Kick-yer-*

*arse Cann'nball.* And I wondered what Mrs Hannibal would be like if we weren't paying.

I'd have liked to talk to Shell about it, but Shell's always thinking about school and people I don't know. She's started riding lessons and Mum took her to buy all the clothes for it. Shell loved it. She put on the whole outfit and showed us all, in the hall last night. She asked Nick if his sisters rode horses, and he said they did. He's got two younger sisters. They go away to boarding school in term-time, too: that's why his house is like a morgue.

Shell twirled round, looking at herself. You could tell she thought the riding clothes were wonderful.

"Do your sisters look like this, when they go riding?" she asked Nick.

"Well, if it's a gymkhana. Most of the time they just crash round in jeans. They think dressing up is a frightful bore."

Shell stopped twirling and looked at him. Then she went to change back into her ordinary clothes. A bit later I saw her on the back kitchen doorstep, scuffing her riding-boots gently against the stone by the side of the door.

"What are you doing, Shell! Mum'll kill you! They're brand-new!"

"They look too new," said Shell. She had some special polish called saddle-soap, and she rubbed it into the scuffed place, then scuffed them a bit more, then rubbed in the polish again. "This is how they ought to look. This is what Corinna's look like."

She wasn't proud of her new riding-clothes any more. Nick had spoiled it for her. I wondered if he'd meant to.

Nick's started me on Latin, and Advanced French. We've got lots of French tapes, as well as books. I'm supposed to listen to them on my Walkman. I like the sound of the Latin better than French. It sounds solid. The words are like tools. They have to fit into the sentences in the right places. Nick says you're all right with Latin, as long as you learn the rules. It doesn't matter about having the right accent. I don't think I'll ever have the right accent in French. When Nick speaks French, he doesn't sound like an English person talking. He's spent every summer in France since he was six.

Nick's been to the sort of school I'm going to. I wonder if all the kids there speak French like he does? I wish I could ask him about it, but he seems to think you know all these things already. He seems to think everybody does. I want to ask him things like what if you can't do your work, do you have to just go on and on all evening, and what if you're ill, and are there locks on the toilets, and is all the food stuff I've never heard of, like spotted dick. And can you phone home. But I haven't asked anything.

I haven't asked him anything for the same reason I haven't been back to look for Sarah Louise. I'm not sure if I want to know or not. All these questions make me feel squeezed-up inside.

It's five o'clock in the evening. I've just finished lessons with Nick. We work from nine to twelve in the morning, then we stop till half-past-two. I go out, to the woods, or up to the horse-chestnuts, or to the old orchard, or down to see the builders. Pete, one of the builders, is really nice. He's a brickie, but he's been out of work. There's not been much building work going on round here, the past six months. But with everything Dad's planning, they'll be working here until next summer. I'm learning a bit about bricklaying. It's a lot harder than it looks. It's a skilled job, Pete says. I like watching him slap on the mortar with his trowel, just enough, nice and easy, then slice it off so the edge of the brickwork is clean. Pete doesn't rush. If you watch him you don't think he's working hard, but at the end of the day you can look back and see a long line of wall he's laid.

"You have to pace yourself," Pete says. He lets me come in the works caravan where they go for tea and a smoke. They've got a meths stove which boils the water. Pete talks to me quite a lot. He was asking me about London yesterday, about jobs on building sites there. I told him Dad would know. I don't tell Pete this, but years ago Dad was on the sites. That was before he went into business. Dad could give him some names, I said.

"I don't want to hang round here for the rest of my life," Pete said. "You get married, have a couple of kids and then you're strapped down for good. Wages're terrible round here. No competition. London's the place if you want the real money."

A wood-pigeon was calling out of the wood. The cement-mixer was still churning, but it wasn't really noisy. Nothing like London.

"It's nice here," I said.

"Nice for a holiday," said Pete. "Not so nice to live. There's no freedom. No buses. You've got to run a car, and that costs money. The women round here think they're lucky if they can get a cleaning job. No choice. You're running to stand still."

He rolled another cigarette and picked up his DAILY MIRROR. I sat in the caravan doorway and watched the drum of the cement-mixer going round and round in the sun.

This afternoon, when we were doing Latin, Nick was talking about the places where they used to speak it. He started telling me about a Roman road which runs through Calverley. There's been an archaeological dig there, and you can see some bits of the road, and some Roman rubbish they've dug up; bits of pots and bones and stuff the Romans threw away. You can learn a lot about people from sifting through their rubbish, even if they are Romans.

Then I thought: *Maybe Nick knows more about this house. When it was built. Who used to live in it.*

So I said, "Nick. A house like this—lots of people would have lived in it, wouldn't they?"

"Oh no. Only one family. It's never been made into flats or anything." Nick's family has always lived round here. He should know about the past.

"But what if there *were* lots of people living here, a long time ago? A hundred years ago?'

*Mr Mord'n. Th'Amiral. Mrs Cann'nball. Mrs Perfeck. Sarah Louise.*

"Well of course there'd be servants," said Nick.

Servants! Of course! Maybe they were all servants, not just Sarah Louise and Mrs Cann'nball, but Mr Mord'n and Mrs Perfeck too. That's what they must have been. You would have had a lot of servants then, in a big house like this.

But what sort of work would Sarah Louise have done? She looks too young and skinny to do much lifting and carrying. And too dirty to do the cooking.

"Nick. What age would they be—servants? I mean, what age would they start? Would you have children being servants?"

Nick laughed. "I'm supposed to be teaching you Latin, not History!"

"But would there? Would they be?"

"I suppose they would. Working in the kitchens or in the gardens in some lowly capacity. Gardener's boy or scullery-maid. And a good thing too. Much better than oiking about in shopping precincts, or whatever

66

they call them. They used to start at the bottom, then if they were any good they'd get trained up."

*They used to start at the bottom.* I could believe that. Like Sarah Louise. She was at the bottom all right.

"D'you think—d'you think they used to get—I mean, beaten up and stuff like that?"

"Good God, *I* don't know! I mean things were different then. People didn't have the same ideas as they do now. They didn't go rushing off to the union every time they wanted a tea-break. And teachers didn't lose their jobs if they laid a finger on the children."

Nick sounded quite angry, so I didn't say anything more. He sounded as if he didn't like the way things were now. Things were different then. Maybe they were. I haven't seen anyone holding a bit of bread the way Sarah Louise did, except on Oxfam posters.

"Anyway," said Nick, "it would have been the Admiral living here in those days. When there was plenty of money for servants."

The Admiral. *Th'Amiral.* Nick doesn't say it like Sarah Louise said it, but it must be the same person. It's got to be.

"Who was the Admiral?"

"Oh, he was a great chap. Self-made man of course." Nick stops and looks at me quickly, but I don't say anything, so he goes on. "He came into a pile of money from somewhere. Nobody really knows anything about it. And he built this place out of it."

"But what was he like?"

"Bit of a rough diamond. But sound enough. My great-grandfather knew him. He was Piers' great-great-grandfather. His great-grandfather came into the house after the Admiral died. He'd been living away with his mother and sister—in some seaside place. Bournemouth, I think. The mother wasn't strong. Lungs, or something like that."

"But the Admiral was here a hundred years ago. How could your great-grandfather have known him?"

"Well, the Admiral lived for a long time after he built the house. He was only about forty-five when he came into the money. He was a bit of a dark horse. But people liked him. He gave a lot of money to the hunt. And round here people remember things. If you ask, they'll reel off everything that's happened since the battle of Trafalgar. You ought to get Mrs H going."

"You mean Mrs Hannibal? Would she know?"

"*Would she know*? Honestly, you're innocent, you city types! Hannibals have been living up in the village since they first came out of the woods. What she doesn't know about Cold Haven isn't worth knowing. Hannibals have always worked here, never mind who owned the house. She knows everyone's business for ten miles round. I just about come within her hunting-grounds. She comes and helps Mum with dinner-parties. You don't need satellite TV if you've got Mrs H."

I wondered if Mrs Hannibal would talk to me the way she talks to Nick. No, she wouldn't. It wouldn't even be worth trying. She likes us to keep out of the way, not dirty her floors, and eat up her meals nicely.

Nick added, casually, "Of course *everyone* round here knows *lots* about you, thanks to Mrs Hannibal. But they still want to know much, *much* more. You wouldn't *believe* the questions people are asking."

I looked down at the page of my Latin book. After a teasing kind of silence, Nick didn't say anything else.

I wish Nick wasn't here. I don't like having a tutor and learning lessons all on my own, the same lessons every time. Latin. French. French. Latin. At my old school we used to do projects, and we could work in groups with our friends.

And I don't like the feeling that Nick is thinking things about us, things Mum and Dad don't know. Mum likes him. She thinks he's all right. But he's not. He must think I'm stupid. He must think I don't understand what he's trying to say when he talks about the Admiral being a 'self-made man'. He's talking about Dad, in a secret kind of way. Hiding what he really means, but saying it just the same.

I wish Dad and Mum wouldn't get back so late from London. I'm in bed by the time they get back, but I always hear them come in. Nick's supposed to be looking after us, but he's in his room, with the door shut, listening to music on his Walkman. He likes the most terrible music. He showed me some tapes. He's always doing things that seem friendly, only they don't feel friendly.

Last night Mum came up to my room. I pretended to be asleep, because it was really late, 11.32 on my watch. Mum sat on the end of the bed, smoking a cigarette. Then she sighed and got up and moved round the room. I looked through a slit of my eyes and she was putting out the cigarette in my washbasin. There was a little hiss as it went out. Then she just stood there, looking up at the sky through a gap in the curtains. I must have fallen asleep before she went.

Three nights ago I was hungry in the middle of the night, so I got up to get a banana or something from downstairs. Mum and Dad were still up. The big sitting-room off the hall, the one that's called the drawing-room, had a light on under the door. I went right up close to it and I could hear voices. Talking, talking. But I couldn't hear what they were saying. The doors here are too thick. At home, I mean in London, I would have just gone in and said I couldn't sleep. But this time I didn't. There was something about the talking which was too serious. It went on and on, on and on. Dad's voice for a long time, then Mum's. I felt cold, so I went back upstairs. It was 2.03 on my watch.

I'm not going to wait any longer. I've decided. Tomorrow, as early as I can, I'm going down to see Sarah Louise.

# Chapter Eight

I've set the alarm on my watch for 6.30. If I get up then, I can go down to the furnace-room without anyone noticing. And I'm so tired. Heavy Latin words thud around my head. MAGister, MAGister, MAGister. It means 'master'.

I fall asleep thinking of the Admiral. The master.

I wake up with a shock just as if the alarm's gone off. But it hasn't. It's still dark. I snap on my bedside lamp and look at my watch. 5.08.

It's cold, too. Half the duvet's fallen off the bed. Maybe that was what woke me up?

No. It wasn't the cold. Now I can hear them again. Voices in the dark, coming from downstairs. I swing my legs out of bed and tiptoe to the door. Then I go back again, and turn out the bedside lamp, in case someone sees light coming through my door when I open it. It's much, much darker than it ever is in London, because there aren't any street-lights, or headlights swinging round the corner through my curtains. But when I open my door, there's a light on downstairs, on Mum and Dad's floor. I peer over the gallery rail. The voice comes again, raised and sharp, a bit like a bird when it's frightened. A bird when you throw a stone into the woods. It's Mum.

I wonder if Shell's woken up too. I look along her side of the landing, but her door's shut, and there's no light under it. Across the railings, on the other side of the wide stairwell, there's a light on. It's under Nick's door. He must have woken up too. But he hasn't opened his door, or come out. Maybe he will though, while I'm standing here.

I don't want him to see me. I creep round the curve of the gallery rail to the stairs, and then look back. Is Nick's door the same as it was? Or has it opened, just a little bit?

I can't hear Mum any more, but I'm frightened. I feel as if something awful is going on. I'm afraid something bad is happening to Mum. She never sounds like that. I tread very softly down the stairs, down to the light. Mum and Dad's floor has a much wider landing than ours. There's a little side-corridor off it, with their bedroom and their bathroom facing. Once I'm there, no-one will be able to see me from upstairs, even if he hangs over the railings.

Mum's left the door open a bit. That's why I could hear them. I stand still, not daring to go any closer. Dad's is the other voice. He's talking quietly, urgently. He must be standing right over by the window, because I can't hear the words properly. But I've got to know. I creep forward over the thick new carpet, and my feet don't make a sound.

" . . . disappear for a bit, that's all . . . "

Then nothing. I can't hear a word. They must be right up close to each other. I hear them say "Paul" through a muddle of words. You know how you always catch your own name when people are talking about you, even when you don't hear what else they're saying.

Suddenly it starts coming through again, clear, like when you move the radio dial and hit the next channel.

Dad's talking. " . . . it'll be the last time, Angie! Then it's finished. Over. I'm getting out of it."

And then Mum, "I still don't like it. I've got a feeling. You've been too lucky."

"What's luck got to do with it? It's *organisation*."

"When'll we know?"

"The last lot's coming through Friday. One more drop, that's all."

"God, I wish it was all over."

"It's the last drop, Angie. It will be, it will be. We'll get it in and out of here in a couple of hours. Friday night, you'll be laughing at yourself."

"Be careful, Micky. You can't mess with these people. They're dangerous. And don't think I don't know you're keeping things from me. I'm not stupid."

"I wouldn't keep things from you, Angie."

"Don't give me that. I don't know what's going on this time. *And I don't want to know*. I just wish to God it was over and we were like we were."

"I'm ahead, Angie, I'm ahead. By the time they catch up with me, it'll all be over. You and I can settle down. Squire and his lady."

And Mum laughs, but not the way she laughs when she's happy. Not the way I can remember her laughing, before any of this started. Before the money and the secrets. Before *business*, and Dad coming back late. And us not asking questions.

> *We're in the money*
> *we're in the money.*

*Go on Paul! Open it! It's a surprise!*
*How about a pony, Shell? What d'you say?*
*Wow! Is it ours? Is it really ours?*
Already I've heard too much. *I just wish to God it was all over and we were like we were.*

73

And so do I. I wish I could talk to Mum. But she's shut off from us too, behind the wall of secrets.

Who are *they*? The ones Dad mustn't mess with? I can guess. It's something to do with the men in cars, the men whose faces you don't see. The men who have the kind of business you don't talk about, not if you know what's good for you. They'd say, "All right sonny?" and ruffle your hair up, but over your head their eyes would be cold as the wind under the door.

I don't want to think about them any more. I don't want to hear any more. I move away from the door, and across the thick carpet, stepping from one dark-red flower to the next, up the stairs, and along our landing. Nick's light is off. But I'm sure he was awake. I think he was listening. I remember what he said: "You wouldn't *believe* the questions people are asking."

Questions about us.

"Who are they?"

"Why've they come here?"

*"Where does all the money come from?"*

How much has Nick heard? Would he understand it if he did hear? I'm not going back to bed. I'll read for a bit, then I'll go out. I want to get out of the house. Everything's muffled here. My feet make a dead sound on the thick stair-carpet. My heart's bumping as if I've been running lap after lap on a race-track, not standing still and stiff outside Mum and Dad's door. I want to get out into the air, where it's cool and fresh and you can hear the wind instead of the whine of the central heating.

I mean to go straight back to my room to get some clothes on, but I find myself going straight past, to Shell's door with the little flowery PRIVATE notice on it. I want to talk to Shell. I'm not going to tell her what I've heard, or what I think it means. I don't want to frighten her, and anyway it makes things seem more real if you tell somebody else about them. I just want to hear her voice. Even if she talks about ponies and ballet, it'll be better than what's going on in my head.

But I hear a different voice. Not Shell's, but a voice coming from me, from the place inside me where I ask questions and know things I don't really want to know.

"*But you promised you were going to see Sarah Louise.*"

Then I hear Sarah Louise's voice: "*Why ent yer come? 'Sdark down 'ere. I ent got no more bread.*" I *am* going to see Sarah Louise! It's just that it's too early. And I've got to get out of the house. I want to be out in the daylight, with Shell talking the way she does, as if everything's OK. Shell talks in a daylight way. I think she's a daylight person. When I'm with Shell, I can stop thinking about the things that belong to the dark.

Shell's funny. She always wakes up straight away, the minute you say her name, and she always knows where she is and what's going on, even if we're staying in a strange house, or she's been asleep in the car. And she doesn't grunt and mutter when she wakes up, the way I do when Mum pulls the duvet off me in the mornings. She thinks in proper sentences right away.

"Paul! Can't you read? It says PRIVATE on my door."

"Listen Shell, I'm going out. D'you want to come? I'm going up to the old orchard. There'll be loads of windfalls after last night."

Shell pushes back her hair. She's growing it, and it's always in her eyes. "All right. But I'll have to have my shower first."

A shower! Just because she's got a shower cabinet in her room. *En suite*, it's called. Shell showers about three times a day now.

"Shell, do me a favour! You don't need a shower!

Just shove your jeans on over your pyjamas. You can get dressed later on."

All right, Shell agrees that she won't have a shower till later. But she's going to get dressed properly, so I'll just have to wait. She makes a noise opening her wardrobe and I hiss at her, "Shut up! They'll hear you!"

" 'Course they won't! They never get up this early."

And I know I can't tell her any of it. She's so calm and so sure everything's OK, as she picks out a sweater from the millions of new sweaters she's got folded up on her wardrobe shelves.

It's starting to get light. I look out of Shell's window and I can see the beginning of the morning, grey, with a bit of red in the sky over the woods. It's still windy, and there are clouds moving fast. There are lots of big black crows walking about on the grass, as if they own the place. Mr Hannibal says deer come right up to the terrace at night, and eat his roses, but I've never seen them. I'd like to see deer. Mr Hannibal says they're pests. Vermin.

"Aren't you going to put your jeans on?" Shell asks.

I look down and find I'm still in my pyjamas. I dodge down the gallery to my own room, and rummage through my drawers to find my clothes. I can't wait to get out. I'm breathing fast, as if there's someone just behind me and I daren't turn round. I cram my feet into trainers without undoing the laces.

Something in Cold Haven is coming alive. Something secret which has been hidden for a long time, waiting.

76

# Chapter Nine

The wet long grass at the side of the path brushes against our jeans legs. My trainers squeak, then they squelch. This part of the garden is wild. Mr Hannibal hasn't got round to it yet. You can't see the house at all from here. And it's so quiet. Just the sounds of wind in the top of the trees, and birds. No people noises at all. There are bushes and little trees leaning out from the sides of the path, snatching at our hair. Everything is tangled together with brambles and white fluffy old man's beard. There are pheasants all round here, in the undergrowth. One of them CRRARKS and there's dead silence, then crackling as they push through the twigs and leaves to get away from us. But we can't see them.

There's a strong, sharp autumn smell. A bonfire smell. All over the path there are little fallen red apples. Mr Hannibal calls them crabs. Shell and I step on them and they split into yellow mush on the path. There are massive spider webs, hanging over the bushes like wet washing. Little parcelled-up flies bounce as we push through the bushes.

"Wait for me, Paul, I'm going to let this one go. It's still alive. I think spiders are horrible."

"Ssh! Don't shout so loud!"

Shell fingers the fly out of the web, but it can't move properly any more. It staggers across her hand. She's broken the web.

"Chuck it away, Shell."

But she won't. She kneels down and puts the fly on a dock-leaf out of the way, where no-one will tread on it. Nobody goes up this path anyway, except me. Mr Hannibal goes up by the road to the kitchen garden.

"Come *on!*"

Now the path is narrow, with clumps of bamboo on one side, and a fence on the other. Mr Hannibal told me they planted the bamboo here years ago, in the Admiral's time. It was planted all down the slope, to hide the cess-pit at the bottom. That's why we're not supposed to play on the bamboos, even though they make brilliant jungle platforms when you bend them over. They grow as thick as broomsticks, five metres high. "You just think what they're feeding on," says Mr Hannibal.

On our left, behind the fence, there are two cottages. Mr Hannibal says one was for the head gardener, and the other was for the keeper. That was when they kept pheasants properly, and had big shoots with people coming down from London for the weekends. But nobody lives in the cottages now. Shell and I went in once, though we weren't supposed to because the floor's in such a bad state you could fall through it. We went up the stairs, leaning against the wall in case the treads were rotten. It smelled dank and musty. It was ghostly in the bedrooms. Sky came in from the wrong places, through gaps in the tiles, and the windows were half-boarded up. It was shadowy. They were tiny bedrooms, two of them, with an iron bed in one of them, and glass on the floor of the other. I told Pete we'd been in there and he told me about a mate of his who smashed his knee up, going through the stairwell of a house. He was a chippy. He hasn't worked since.

Everything I know about Cold Haven comes from people who've always lived round here. I know the house is ours, but it doesn't feel like it. We've only just come, but it's always been part of their lives. They know who planted the trees, who started to dig a well and gave up, who got drunk one night and split his head open on the gateposts. That really happened. It was Mr Hannibal's father, one night, after he'd fallen out with the gamekeeper.

The cottages are going to be done up. But it's dark in this part of the garden. Grounds, I mean. I wouldn't want to live up here. I didn't even feel like trying to make a den in the cottages. It was too empty and sad in there.

But just here the path broadens and splits, and light comes in. You can go up past the greenhouses and the kitchen garden, or down to the chestnut grove. They're sweet chestnuts, the kind you can eat. Spanish chestnuts, Mr Hannibal calls them. I wear my gloves to split the cases open, then I cook them over a campfire. It's great up by the sweet chestnuts. There are squirrels all over the place, and they're not frightened of people at all. They look at you, then they carry on scrabbling around with their nuts. They don't leave many for humans. But then I suppose it's their place really.

We take the path down. I'd like to go up to the kitchen garden, but there isn't time if we're going to get the windfalls before breakfast. The kitchen garden has a high wall all round it, made of soft red bricks, and it has a squeaky iron gate so that you can't get in without Mr Hannibal knowing, if he's working up there. Outside the kitchen garden there are little flower gardens, with low hedges round them, where he grows flowers for cutting. Some go to the house and some he sells. I've seen him wobbling off with a great load of dahlias flopping over his handlebars.

Then there are the long glasshouses, always warm and dry and full of dead wasps and flies which can't get out again once they've flown in. There's nothing growing in them now. The wooden doors don't fit properly, and all the paint is blistering and peeling.

I love it up there by the glasshouses. It's warm, and it feels as if the sun's trapped there, even on a dull day. It's a secret place. There's a pear tree with long green pears hanging by the wall, and another tree called a medlar tree, which has fruit which look a bit like squashed-up pears. Only when you bite into them, they're so sour all your spit dries up. Mr Hannibal says you have to let them stay on the tree until they're half-rotten. Then they're bletted, and you can eat them. People would pay good money for well-bletted medlars, years ago, up in the London markets, but they've lost the taste for them now.

But now we go down the path through the sweet chestnuts. There's the wall. It's crumbling and falling down. You can climb through to the bottom of the Old Orchard. It's called the old orchard because the new orchard is inside the kitchen garden. The Old Orchard lies between the kitchen garden wall and the woods. The woods are wilder than anywhere else. You can't get through them for briars and brambles. You have to keep to the track.

The new orchard, inside the kitchen garden, is neat and looked after. The grass is cut short under the trees. All the trees are quite small, and some of them grow in lines with their branches spread out on wires. There are fat little pear trees, and lots of different kinds of apples. We've had the early sorts, but all the late ones are still on the trees. Each tree has a label.

*Egremont Russet. James Grieve. Beurre Hardy. Comice. Conference.* There aren't any surprises in the new orchard. I like it, but it feels as if it belongs to Mr Hannibal. He's always in the kitchen garden. That's what he likes best. When I'm there, I feel as if he's waiting for me to go, so that he can have it to himself again.

We aren't supposed to pick the fruit there, because if you do it wrong, it damages the crop for next year. Mr Hannibal does the picking. I've seen him. He weighs an apple in his hand, lifts it, gives a little twist to the stem, and it's picked.

"If it's ripe, it'll come off easy. Yer don't need ter pull at it." He lays the apples in flat baskets and brings them into the house.

There's a fig tree on the west wall, and peach trees all along the south wall. The grape-house hasn't got a vine in it now, though. The vine got a disease and it had to be burnt, then Mr Hannibal smoked out the grape-house to kill off the vine fungus. He says he's always managed to keep up the kitchen garden and the new orchard. But he had to let the Old Orchard go. It was too much for one man.

The kitchen garden catches all the sun. It smells of fruit and green leaves and the muck Mr Hannibal spreads on the beds he's going to use next year. But the Old Orchard is the best place in Cold Haven. When I'm there, I don't want to go back to London any more. I hope it stays the way it is for ever. I hope Dad doesn't get a team of men in to clear it, the way Mr Hannibal wants him to.

You climb over the wall, and you're in. The ground's higher on the other side, nearly level with the wall. I've made some paths, but most of the orchard is covered with high banks of brambles which must have been growing there for years and years. They've joined up with each other and even in the clear spaces there are tall weeds, mostly purple, and creepers, and fallen branches which have gone rotten. The Old Orchard smells of apples, fresh apples and fallen apples and mushrooms growing on the underside of branches which have blown down in gales. It smells of leaves and foxes and ripe blackberries. Some of the trees are covered with ivy, and they're so old they've hardly got any leaves, and no fruit at all. The fungus makes lace patterns on their branches.

I think Mr Hannibal must come in and chop the undergrowth back sometimes. Once I saw a ladder leaning against a tree, and the next day it was gone. And some of the trees look young and healthy, as if they haven't been planted all that long ago.

I found a dead vole here one day, with five little pink baby voles squirming round it. I put them in a box and tried to feed them milk out of the dropper in my chemistry set, but they all died by the end of the day. Some of the trees have got so much grey lacy stuff growing over them that you can pick it off in sheets.

The Old Orchard is my place. Nobody else comes here. You can do what you like.

I've made some paths by bashing down the brambles with a stick, and cutting through them with a pair of secateurs I bought up in Calverley. But it takes ages. In some parts you can crawl from one tree to another. The smell of foxes is as strong as it is round the bins in London. I haven't seen a fox yet, but one day I'm going to come up here while it's still dark, and see if I can watch them playing at dawn. I've seen a slow-worm, and pheasants, and loads of rabbits.

Shell's only been up here once. She isn't really interested in the kitchen garden or the Old Orchard. She likes the field where the horses are. She's making a tree-house down there. It's supposed to be private, for her to go in with her friends.

I always come back to the same place in the Old Orchard. There's a tunnel between two apple trees which have their branches growing right down to the ground. They drop huge apples, sour ones with bright green skins. But they taste good if you roast them in a fire and put sugar on them. I've got sugar and matches and stuff wrapped in a plastic bag, hidden under the tree. It's all right to light fires up here, now the ground's so wet, as long as it's nowhere near the trees. I haven't really asked Mr Hannibal if it's OK, but he sort of knows about it. Anyway, he sees the smoke.

You crawl through the tunnel, and you come out facing one of the biggest apple trees in the old orchard. And all the trees are big. It's a round tree, like apple trees in pictures, and it's covered all over with red apples. They're the only really red apples in the whole orchard. They're not shiny, but they glow from inside, against the dark leaves. And they're a good size too. Lots of apples up here are small, because the trees haven't been looked after for years. All their strength has gone into growing tall and wild.

I'm sure these apples are eating apples. They're so bright, and smooth, and round. When I look at them, I can nearly taste them. I know the way the juice will burst out when I bite in through their skins. But it's impossible to get anywhere near the tree. I keep trying. I've tried every time I've been up here, but I just get ripped and scratched by brambles until I have to go back.

So now Shell and I stand there with a bank of brambles as high as my shoulders between us and the red apple tree. I've tried slashing through with my secateurs, but the brambles are so thick and they're all twisted over each other, and they claw your face and hands. You'd need a flame-thrower.

"Maybe there's another way round," says Shell.

I don't think there is, but we can try. We go back a bit and start trampling our way over the weeds and creepers and thorns. They aren't quite as high just here. If we had boots on we could smash them down, but it hurts through trainers. I wish I'd brought my secateurs. Or a knife.

Shell finds a heavy bit of fallen branch and bashes a bit of a pathway through with it. But we aren't getting any closer. We're just going in a circle round the tree. It stands there, like a person. It holds up its arms full of apples as if it's waiting for us. But it won't help us. We have to find the way for ourselves.

Suddenly, down the other end of the orchard, a black tangle of crows whirls up screaming from a big pear tree. Something's frightened them.

It can't be us. We're too far away. And it's too early for anyone else. Mr Hannibal comes at eight, and the builders don't start till then either. And there's nobody else.

But I can't see anything. The orchard's huge, and it's so overgrown I've never got down to the end of it. I don't like to go too far down. I get a sort of light, frightened feeling in the back of my legs when I'm deep in the orchard. But I know it joins on to the wood.

Somebody could get in through the wood. Somebody could have got in through the wood. You can get to the wood without ever going near the house. There's a little road running along the bottom of the fields, and a gate off it, and a lane which runs up through the wood. No-one uses the lane, but it gets cleared sometimes. You could get up that way. No-one would see you.

Shell stands very still. The crows swoop low, and

scream, then rise again. She looks at me. A small, sideways look. A scared look. She feels the same as I do. A long way from the house, on our own.

I put my finger on my lips. She nods. I point backwards, the way we've come. Just back there, there's another tunnel, going the other way, away from the red apple tree. It goes back towards the kitchen garden wall. We can't climb the wall there, because it's too high, but maybe we can make our way along to the corner. There's a step up there and a sort of stile place where the brick wall joins an old stone wall. Once we are through there we'd be safe. Then we could easily get out through the kitchen garden gate. We could run. Here, you can't. When you try to move fast it's like running in dreams.

Shell lays her fallen branch down on the grass without making a sound. As lightly as we can, we ease our way back along the path we've just made by pushing through.

"Craa—craa—" The birds call and circle. They won't settle. Whatever's disturbed them is still there.

A bramble catches Shell's jacket and grips her. It won't let go. She can't get at it, and for a moment she's frantic, tugging at it, her eyes wild in a white face. I get hold of her and unhook the bramble's tough claw. She ducks down and round the next tangle. Behind us, the crows are still up in the air. They are angry. We stop and listen. Nothing. Silence except for the crows. Then a cracking, crackling sound, a long way away.

It could be a branch dropping. After last night's wind. And those big apples make a lot of noise when they thump down through all the undergrowth.

But I don't think so. I think it's the sort of crackling noise you get when something's moving. Or someone. Maybe more than open person. Moving forward steadily and stealthily. Not making much noise. And knowing nobody'll notice, because they are out of sight of the house.

Here's the tunnel. Quick. This time I go first, because Shell's never been down here. It's only a narrow tunnel and you have to crawl over brown rotting apples with white mould on them. The tunnel smells like a pub with its door open when you go past. I shove the apples out of the way so Shell won't have to crawl over them. My fingers sink into their rottenness. Shell hates things like that. But I don't mind. They're only apples.

We're up to the wall. But where the tunnel used to run straight through, alongside the wall, there's a huge pile of branches and leaves and garden rubbish. The pile's about six foot high and it blocks the tunnel completely. We can't go round it, because the brambles are even worse here. And there'll be too much noise if we start shifting this lot. Mr Hannibal must have dumped it over the wall.

We'll have to go back. But not the way we came. Maybe down here. Try this space. It might lead into a path. I'm soaked from the wet grass now but I don't feel cold. I feel boiling, and my heart's beating so hard I'm sure Shell can hear it.

"I think we can get round this way," I whisper back to her.

She wipes her hair off her pale face. She's dirty and there's blood on her cheek where a bramble's scratched her. But she's OK. She nods.

I can't crawl any more. The branches are too low. But if I lie down, and wriggle on my stomach, I can get through. And round this corner the path widens. We're not going the right way, not if we want to get back to the kitchen garden, but there isn't any other way. A spider's web catches across my face, warm and clinging. I brush it off but it won't go away. It sticks on my lips like candyfloss. Now the path's getting wider again. The undergrowth's so thick I can't see anything to the sides of us, but ahead there's an opening, and grass, short grass, and streaks of sun.

And we're through. It isn't sun, just white daylight. I stand up, and it hurts after crawling for so long. And right in front of us is a thick black tree trunk. We look up and we see the undersides of leaves which are going yellow and crisp at the edges, and the undersides of red apples, dark as cherries against the plain morning sky.

We've made it. We've reached the tree. The secret tree that no-one else has ever reached. But how did we do it? There are still bramble banks all around, but we're on the other side of them, on the side of the tree.

I watch Shell's hand go up as if in slow motion, and touch one of the apples. She weighs it in her hand. It's big, bigger than Shell's hand. Then she lifts it and twists the stalk a little and the ripe apple comes away. She looks for a dry patch on her wet muddy jeans, and she rubs the apple until it shines. Daylight flickers on the polished apple. Then she lifts it to her mouth.

"Don't, Shell!" I say sharply. She turns, apple poised in her hand, mouth open. Why did I say that?

She looks at me calmly: "Why not?" she asks, and opens her mouth and takes a big bite out of the apple.

I reach up and touch the nearest apple. There isn't any wind at all now, and the fruit hang perfectly still on their twigs. Why not? I feel the weight, as Shell did, and take the apple.

It fizzes in my mouth and the juice runs down the bitten part onto my sweatshirt. The taste is sharp and fresh, not very sweet. I look at where I've bitten. The flesh of the apple isn't white. It's a creamy colour with little red veins running through it, like human veins. I don't finish it. I walk round the tree, choosing apples. Six of the reddest, most perfectly shaped, with their stalks still on. I take off my sweatshirt and tie the apples into it, so I can carry them and they won't get bruised.

They're not for me. They're for Sarah Louise. She's hungry.

"Paul!" whispers Shell. "Listen!"

It's a car. A car engine starting. But the sound's coming from the wrong direction. Our cars start over by the garages. Sometimes a car comes down the road from Calverley, but that's behind us. This car is starting where there isn't a road. And it's quite near. The cough of an engine. Like someone clearing his throat.

There isn't a road. But there's the track, the little lane that leads up from the bottom road by the field. Nobody uses it, and there's grass growing all over it, and wild rose bushes nearly meet overhead. Maybe the track comes all the way up to the orchard. You could drive up it if you had the right sort of vehicle. Something tough, with a four-wheel-drive. A jeep, maybe. I can't tell from the engine noise.

The engine revs. It's making a lot of noise. It must be reversing down the track through the woods, away from us. There isn't room to turn.

They've gone.

Shell turns to me. "I don't like it here, Paul. I want to go home."

"It's all right. They've gone. We can go back to the wall, and clear the stuff and get through that way. It doesn't matter if we make a noise now."

"Can you put my apples in with yours, Paul?"

I tie in Shell's apples. I wonder if we'll ever come back and pick the rest of the treeful?

"Shell. Who d'you reckon it was? With the car?"

A closed look comes over Shell's face. I should've known it was no good asking her. "I expect it was just someone who went the wrong way. We were stupid getting frightened."

Yeah. Trust Shell. Ask no questions. Ask no questions and you'll be told no lies.

"Shell. Listen. Let's go and see."

Why did I say that? I don't want to see. I want to run home and shut the door and never come back here again. But . . .

The smell of the Old Orchard is all round me. I think of campfires, and the little voles. I want to be able to come back. I don't want to be too frightened to come back.

"They must've come for something. They wouldn't come all this way for nothing. Please, Shell."

She looks at me, and says in a voice I can hardly hear, "D'you think they've gone back to London now?"

And I nod. She's right, I'm sure of it. Whoever they are, they don't belong here. They come at night, or very early in the morning, when no-one's around. They don't want to be seen. And it's best for you if you never see them. I shiver.

Shell stands there. I don't know if she's going to come with me, and I can't go on my own. I'm thinking inside fiercely, "C'm *on*, c'm *on*."

Then she steps forward.

# Chapter Ten

I can't help it. I yawn. A huge stretchy yawn which makes my eyes water. The tight, frightened feeling in the air snaps, and Shell laughs in a way I haven't heard her laugh since we came to Cold Haven.

"We'd better get on with it before you fall asleep!" she says cheekily.

"It's all right for *you*. I've been up for hours."

"You're probably hungry. You know what you're like if you go without breakfast."

Now that she says it, I realise I'm starving. I think of toast. Thick slices of toast with butter soaking into the top, and a scraping of marmite. I think of a tall cold glass of orange juice. I swallow hard.

Then I think of Sarah Louise's face. That's what starving means. Pinched and big-eyed, but patient; waiting for me and believing I'll come back because I said I would. The apples bump against my chest. *Hold on*, I say silently, *I'm coming back. But first I've got to find out what's happening.* And suddenly I have the strangest feeling that Sarah Louise knows. She's still down in the passage under the house, but in a way she's here with me. She knows what I'm thinking.

We burrow back through paths and tunnels. I don't feel frightened now, and I don't think Shell does either.

It might be because I'm tired or because I haven't had anything to eat, but nothing feels quite sharp and real any more.

We work our way down the orchard. Soon I'm on new ground, where I've never been before. It's wild, but we can get through. And I'm sure parts of it have been cleared. Yes, these branches have been chopped back. And the cuts are new. They haven't healed over yet. Someone has been down here, clearing the orchard. Dad didn't say anything about it. Why didn't he tell me?

"Where d'you think they were?" Shell whispers.

We look around. The orchard slopes slightly towards the woods, so we are lower now than we were when we heard the car. The wood is near and dark. And there, like an open mouth, is the lane. The gate between the orchard and the lane is pulled right back. It's an old gate, rickety and covered with lichen. They must have had to lift it and drag it. The long grass has been mashed down by tyres. The tyre marks are new and there are deep ruts where the tyres have spun and gripped in the wet ground. It must have been a jeep. A car couldn't have got through. This is the place where it stopped. This is where they got out. The tyre marks are deeper just here, where the jeep must have started to reverse back to the gate.

The grass has been battered down by rain and wind. It's hard to spot boot tracks.

Shell walks backwards slowly. Suddenly she dips down.

"What is it?"

"Fag-end. Look." She holds it up. It's fresh, not soaked through by the night's rain. So they *were* here. They got out of the jeep and walked up this way. Why?

"Leave it, Shell. Put it back where it was."

Shell keeps on walking backwards. I follow. She

points to a crushed clump of grass. Then another. Then a patch of mud with a slurred print in it.

The long grass gives way to undergrowth. Someone's done what we wanted to do earlier. The brambles are bent and smashed by heavy boots. Then there's a little clearing with a tree in it. Not a fruit tree. It's a sycamore that's grown out of a helicopter seed blown over from the woods. And under it there's a dark green patch like a cushion of moss. But it's not.

"Don't touch it!" says Shell. She grabs my hand. We shrink back, thinking of bombs in rubbish bins, neatly packed, looking harmless.

This is just a neat green canvas packet, securely tied. It's about the size of my school backpack. It might be part of a camper's gear. It might be anything.

"It can't be a bomb," I say. "Who'd put a bomb down here just to give the old crows a shock?"

Shell's hand relaxes in mine. "What d'you think it is?" she asks.

"I dunno. Could be anything."

"Paul—what if it's jewels?"

Jewels! Just like an adventure story. That means it can't be. But I look at Shell and I see diamonds and rubies glowing in her eyes. She wants it to be magical.

"All right," I say, "I'll have a quick look."

"No, you mustn't! What if they find out? They'll guess it's us! There's no-one else round here."

"I'll do it so they can't tell. See the way it's lying? We'll put it back just the same. I won't even lift it. I'll just sort of untie it and roll it over."

"What about your fingerprints?"

What about my fingerprints? I glance admiringly at Shell. I hadn't thought of that. Shell's so quiet I sometimes forget how quick she is.

"Hang on. I'll take off my t-shirt and wrap up my hand in that, then there won't be any."

I strip off my t-shirt. I've already used my sweatshirt to carry the apples, so now I've just got my jeans on and I'm freezing. Shell pulls off her sweater. "Here, you can have this. I've got a vest on as well as my t-shirt."

Her sweater is much too small for me, but it's warm and I'm glad of it. Luckily there's no-one here to see me wearing a sweater with a butterfly design on the front. I wind my t-shirt around my hand so that I can still move my fingers to undo the parcel, and I kneel down on the grass. Shell stands just behind me.

The parcel feels firm, but not hard. There's a fiddly buckle, then velcro tabs. Easy. I pull back the flap.

Inside there's a square packet wrapped round in opaque polythene. It's sealed at the corners. You can't open it without tearing the polythene. And if I do that, they'll know someone's been here. I touch the packet. It gives way a little. Whatever's in it isn't that hard. And it's not heavy either. I feel along the packet. There are little ridges, as if there's more packing inside, more little hidden parcels. I can't see through the polythene at all.

Shell's breath is on my neck. "What is it? Can't you open it?"

I show her. "I can't open it without tearing it. It's been heat-sealed. Look."

We both stare at the packet, frustrated. But in a little part of my mind I'm relieved. We can't open it. It's not our fault that we don't know what's in it. And we don't have to do anything about it. We can go home.

Quickly, carefully, I pack up the canvas and fix the tabs and the buckle. Suddenly it feels dangerous again. Someone cared a lot about this parcel. So much that they drove up here at dawn, using the track through the woods so no-one would see them. And maybe, whoever that someone is, he or she will be coming back. And I don't think it's just one someone. There'd be a driver, a person to keep watch, another to hide the packet. Three at least, and maybe more.

There's a click in the branches above us. We stare up.

A blackbird is looking at us with her head on one side. She's a brown female. I wonder if she watched while *they* hid the packet? She might know what they look like. She might have heard what they said.

But she isn't going to tell us. She watches us sideways out of her bright hard eye, then she bounces off her perch and flies away.

# *Chapter Eleven*

It would have been all right if I hadn't dropped the apples. The knot I'd tied in my sweater must've slipped, because out they rolled, one after another, thud, thud, thud, on the polished hall floor, skidding under the monks' table, idling there, rocking just out of reach. Shell and I were scrabbling under the table when a voice floated over the gallery rail, right down from the second floor. A lazy, teasing voice, not too loud. Nick.

"Good Lord! Have you two been scavenging again? Doesn't Mrs H give you enough to eat? I'll have to have a word with her."

I won't look up. I wriggle round and find the last apple by the table leg. All the apples are bruised and one of them's split open.

Nick's coming downstairs.

*"Don't say anything!"* I whisper to Shell.

She tosses back her hair and rolls her eyes. Of course she won't. She never says the wrong thing.

"Here. You take yours," I say, more loudly, but still being careful because of Mum and Dad. And I divide the apples up to give Shell her share. But she doesn't want them any more.

"You can have them," she says. "They're all bruised

now. I was going to take them to school and give them to my friends."

Nick's at the bottom of the stairs, crossing the hall. He looks wide-awake and pleased with himself. I'm sure he's been up for hours. Snooping around. Listening. He strolls over to us.

"Looks as if you found a good place to go scrumping," he says. "I don't remember Hannibal bringing any of those in yesterday. They're beauties."

"We weren't scrumping. They're ours," said Shell in a flat voice. She sounds as if she doesn't like Nick, either. I thought she did. Maybe she's noticed the way he says things and then pretends they're just jokes. Things about us. Maybe she's noticed how he looks down on us.

"Yes, of course they are," says Nick, very politely now. "Can I have one?"

"They're all bruised from falling on the floor," says Shell, and she reaches over to the fruitbowl and picks him out one of the big Charles Ross apples Mr Hannibal brought in yesterday. She makes a show of picking out the best one, and Nick has to take it. It's enormous. He could make a pudding out of it, I think to myself. One of those school puddings he likes so much.

Shell is brilliant sometimes. The way she gives the apple to Nick. It couldn't be clearer if she'd said out loud, *Everything here belongs to us. I can give you apples if I want to. But I'll choose what kind.* She really doesn't like him. Great. Things are getting better all the time.

"Too early for brekker, I suppose," says Nick. He wanders towards the main kitchen. "I'll scrounge around and see what's on offer."

Brekker! Shell rolls her eyes at me again. I make a mad face back. It's still only 7.32. But it seems like weeks since I woke up. The apples weigh heavy. Juice is making my sweater damp as it seeps out of the splits and bruises.

It's still early. I could go down now and give them to Sarah Louise. It's risky, with Nick around listening and spying. But maybe . . .

"Shell. Listen. Do something for me? Please! It's important."

"All right."

"Keep Nick out of the way. Just for half-an-hour. Take him off somewhere. Take him down to the horses."

"But I've got to change before school." Shell looks down at herself. She's wet and muddy and her face is even worse, with a mixture of blood and blackberry juice smeared over one cheek. But luckily she can't see that.

"Just for ten minutes then. *Go on.*"

Shell looks as if she's going to ask questions, but she doesn't. She just says, "OK," and the next minute she's run into the kitchen and I hear her say to Nick, "Hey Nick! Can you take me down to see the horses?"

She sounds totally different from how she sounded before. She sounds like Nick's her favourite big brother. And amazingly, Nick doesn't see that it's all put on. And I hear Nick's voice, pleased and warm. Maybe he does really like Shell after all. A couple of minutes later they swing through the hall together, Shell hanging onto Nick's arm, chattering about horses, looking up at Nick with the big-brother look on her face as well as in her voice.

"Paul, if Mum gets up, tell her Nick's taken me down to the horses."

And the door shuts. They're out of the way.

And I'm into the main kitchen in seconds. I grab Dad's car torch from by the back-door, though we're not supposed to touch it, and I'm through the invention

97

room (which was really called a scullery, Nick says), through the cellar door, down the steps, across and into the passage.

It's funny how the passage feels warmer than the furnace-room. As if there's warm air blowing through from somewhere. It smells coaly, too.

As soon as I get round the corner I know it's all right. All the things I've been thinking, about grey bundles of rags lying still on the floor, go out of my mind in a puff of relief. There's Sarah Louise, sitting cross-legged, frowning with concentration. She throws up a smooth big pebble and scoops up a lot of little pebbles while it's still in the air. Then she looks up and sees me and grins.

"'Ello! Yer 'ere agen! *That* din take long!"

Didn't take long! She must have been ill again. It's six days now since I came down here. Maybe she's had a temperature and the time's sort of blurred in her mind.

But she had my watch.

"Sarah Louise. What's the time?"

She looks down at the watch, which she's strapped round her wrist. But it's too big, because she's too thin.

"I carn read, can I?" she asks in a cross voice.

Oh.

"Let me have a look."

I shine the car torch onto the watch. It's a big powerful beam of light, much stronger than my torch.

The watch says 11.59. I flip the date-button, and read. 13.2.1892.

"Give the watch here a minute," I say.

"Yer giv it me. Yer said yer giv it me."

"Yeah, I know I did, I'm not taking it. I just want to have a look. I think it's gone wrong."

Sarah Louise undoes the watch and I take it. Now

98

I'm holding it again I wish I hadn't given it to her. It's much better than my other one. I have to wear my old one now, the one I had before we were in the money. I hold it up and shine the torch on it. I press the buttons and this time it reads: 7.46. And the date button shows: 27.10.1992.

The watch is showing one time when it's on Sarah Louise's wrist, and another time when I'm holding it. What does it mean? Maybe Sarah Louise was right. Maybe it *is* February. Maybe it *is* a hundred years ago. But only for her, not for me.

"Djer get me any a yer sanwiches?"

I remember the apples. I untie the sweater, and pick out the best I can find. It's a bit bruised, but not very. And it's so red it seems to shine, even down here. I hold it out to Sarah Louise, and I hold my breath. Will it disappear, like the food I brought before, and the milk?

The apple goes safely into her hand. It looks as if it belongs there. The apples belong to Cold Haven, and Sarah Louise belongs to Cold Haven. The apple tree was secret and hidden away, just like Sarah Louise, and yet we got to it, just like I found Sarah Louise. I don't really understand how either of those two things happened. I won't think about it now. I'll think about it later, when I'm on my own. Her skinny grip fastens round the apple. She doesn't take a big bite. She sort of gnaws at the skin, not ever taking her teeth out of it, like a dog does when it finds something in the dustbin. Juice runs down her chin, and little bits of apple poke out of the corners of her mouth. Sarah Louise sucks the core dry, and lays it carefully in her lap, as if she might need it. Then she looks at me, and for the first time I hear her laugh.

"I know where yer bin thievin'! Yer bin up th'Orchid,

ent yer? Yer wanter watch Mr 'Annibal dunt ketch yer, thievin' in 'is new orchid."

I suppose the Old Orchard must've been new, a hundred years ago. That would have been long before they planted the other trees in the kitchen garden. How long do apple trees live? Could the red apple tree have been there in Sarah Louise's time?

"I've got you some more. Here." I give Sarah Louise the rest of the apples. She looks at each one, rubs it on her shawl, and tucks it carefully away. I wonder if she's still got any of her bread left.

"How long have you been down here?" I ask.

"I dunno. I bin ill. When yer come this mornin', didjer see *her*? Is she lookin' for me?"

It's no good telling Sarah Louise it's been six days since I was down here. "D'you mean Mrs Cann'nball?" I ask.

"Yeah. *Her*. I bin listenin', but I din 'ear anythin'."

I remember how Sarah Louise was listening, looking up at the roof, up where the kitchen is.

"Mindjer," goes on Sarah Louise, "yer carn 'ear Mrs Cann'nball 'f she doan want yer ter 'ear 'er. She steps light, for all she's so big."

A picture forms in my mind. Mrs Cannonball, plump and light as a cat, moving silently around the house. "Maybe they think you've gone. I mean, gone right away. Away from Cold Haven. Maybe they aren't looking for you any more."

For a moment Sarah Louise brightens, then she says, "No. That's not 'er way. She'll be waitin', just like a cat by an 'ole, waitin' for a mouse."

I see it as Sarah Louise says it. It's the same as it was up in the orchard. It's as if Sarah Louise is in among my own thoughts. She can make me see things, even if I don't want to. Mrs Cann'nball, in her dark greasy dress with her big arms like legs of lamb from a freezer, tiptoeing across the furnace-room floor and waiting, waiting. She wouldn't mind waiting. She'd enjoy it just the way a cat enjoys catching a mouse, playing with it, letting it think it's got away, then putting a paw down on it again.

And the others. The rest of *them*. Mr Mord'n. Tall, with white slippery hands. Bowing at people upstairs. Taking their coats and smiling. Coming down rubbing his hands together. Coming down to talk to Mrs Cann'nball in a voice nobody can overhear. A soft voice, slippery like his hands. Mr Mord'n.

Mrs Perfeck. Fat and rosy in a white crackling apron. Keys round her waist. Bustling and swishing down the corridors. You wouldn't think she was frightening at all.

Unless . . .

. . . unless you were just going down the back stairs and you slipped with a jug of hot water and it spilled and the jug broke and Mrs Perfeck was at the top of the stairs with her white apron and she looked down at you, face like death, and said in a tight mincy voice over her shoulder, "It's nothing, sir. Just one of the girls." And she shut the back stairs door and you saw the white apron shooing down to get you, flapping in your face, blinding you. The white apron and the red face and the low hissing voice, "Get yourself down them stairs. Impidence. Yer belong in the back kitchen and don't forget it."

And you stumbled back down the stairs blabbering: "I were only just 'elpin Rose. She's 'ert 'er arm."

"'Ert 'er arm! I'll give yer 'ert 'er arm."

"Doan 'it me! Doan 'ert me!"

*I can see them all. I can hear them all. Is it something Sarah Louise is doing to me? Is Sarah Louise making me see them?*

The old days Nick was talking about in our Latin

lesson. The old days Nick likes. *Things were different then. People didn't have the same ideas as they do now.* People like Nick had things the way they liked. They rang for hot water and tea and whatever else they wanted. They threw their dirty clothes down on the floor for someone to take them away. They pointed out a smear of polish on the furniture, making a joke of it so Mrs Perfeck went downstairs with a face like thunder, a storm ready to break on Sarah Louise.

People who owned big houses like Cold Haven. People like us.

The Admiral. What was he like? Sarah Louise is frightened of him, too.

She doesn't look frightened now though. She's playing her game again, with the big stones and the little stones. It's like jacks. And she's singing too:

> *"Poor Jenny sits a weepin'*
> *a weepin' a weepin'*
> *poor Jenny sits a weepin'*
> *on a bright summer's DAY"*

and as she sings DAY she throws the stones up in the air and catches them on the back of her hand:

> *"an' WHY is she weepin'*
> *weepin' weepin' . . . ?"*

Shell knows that song. Only she doesn't sing songs like that any more. I like the way Sarah Louise sings it. She doesn't look sad when she's singing, even when she comes to the bit about a bright summer's day. I wonder how long it is since Sarah Louise has seen the sun.

"Are yer comin' back agen?" Sarah Louise asks me, tossing up her handful of stones.

I haven't even said I'm thinking about going back upstairs, but she can tell. "I'll come back. And I'll help you. I'll help you to get out, away from *them*. I won't be long."

But Sarah Louise doesn't seem to be listening to me any more. She's still singing her song. I hear it until I'm at the end of the passage, then it stops as if someone's sliced through it with a knife.

# Chapter Twelve

Why could Sarah Louise eat the apple, but not the sandwiches? I still think it's something to do with belonging. Sarah Louise belongs here, and the apples belong here. They are all connected somehow, in a way I can't understand. But my sandwiches and milk didn't belong to Cold Haven. They were just stuff Mum had bought in the supermarket. What about the watch? Sarah Louise can wear my watch. She can even make it change to her own time. But time is hard to think about. Because I'm alive NOW, I think time belongs to me. I think I am NOW and everything else is THEN. But Sarah Louise doesn't think that. She thinks she is NOW. And what does that make me?

I try to work it out as I go up the stairs to my room, but I'm too tired. My legs hurt at the back after all the crawling through the orchard, and my head aches. There's fluff in the corner of the stairs, the kind of fluff that comes off brand-new carpets.

Dad opens the bedroom door, looks across, and sees me. "You're an early bird, Paulie," he says in a bright voice.

"Been out in the garden," I mumble, hoping that if I look down and keep close to the wall he won't see the mess I'm in. But I needn't worry. Dad isn't really looking at me. He's got a blank, whistling look fixed on his face. Like a grinning Hallowe'en mask which is only frightening because it looks so much like a real person, and yet it isn't. I want to tear the mask off him. I want to shout at him, "Dad! Dad! I know you're in there! Come out!"

But I say nothing.

Dad rubs his hands over his cheeks where he's just shaved, as if he's surprised to find how smooth they are. In fact he looks as if he's surprised to find himself there at all.

"Is Mum all right?" I ask. It just bursts out before I can stop myself.

Dad laughs. " 'Course she's all right!" Then he seems to think of something and his face goes serious. He *makes* his face go serious. You can see him choosing to do it, then a minute afterwards his face does what it's been told. "Well, tell you the truth, Paul, she's not feeling too great this morning. So you and Shell be good, eh? One of these bugs going round, I daresay. So be a sensible boy and let her have a lie-in."

"But what about Shell? Mum's got to take her to school. There aren't any buses here."

Dad stops again. He frowns really painfully, as if I've just told him something terrible. Something he hasn't planned for. He must've forgotten all about Shell.

"Yeah. Of course. Shell. Right. Tell her to get moving and I'll take her in."

"Where're you going, Dad?"

"Just a bit of business again, Paul. Same old story eh? Be good now. Help your mum."

He says that in a quick, *'don't bother me now'* voice, but then as he goes past me and on down the stairs something different happens. He stops, turns back, and sort of grabs me, awkwardly, so that for a moment

105

we sway and I think I'm going to fall down the stairs on top of him. But I don't. He hugs me tight, really tight. I can't remember Dad hugging me like that for years, not since I fell off my bike when I was eight and a car had to swerve to miss me and Dad came running over and picked me up off the road. Dad feels hot, burning hot, as if he's got a temperature.

I say, "Oh Dad, Dad," and I think I'm going to cry.

Then he lets go and turns away so I can't see his face. He starts to say something but then he changes his mind and just puts his hand on my shoulder and shakes it quite hard so I can feel his fingers pressing into me. It's hard to believe, but I think Dad might have been going to cry too. Then he turns away and runs down the stairs, fast, shouting for Shell.

I don't go after him. I feel so tired now that I just climb up the stairs to our floor, push open the door of my room and collapse on top of the duvet in my muddy jeans and Shell's sweater. In a minute I'll take them off and go and have a shower and put on something dry and warm. I shut my eyes and darkness whirls in front of me. I want to lift my head but I can't. I can hear someone singing.

It's 15.04 when I wake up, and the house is silent. I am cold and stiff and aching, but I feel much better. I've been asleep for seven whole hours in the day-time—I've never done that before. I wonder if Nick's been looking for me? We ought to have been doing lessons. Maybe he's been in here while I was asleep. I don't like the thought of that.

My jeans have dried on me, stiff and cardboardy with mud. I don't know what to do with them so I roll them up tight with Shell's sweater and my socks and shove them into the back of the wardrobe, where Mrs Hannibal won't find them. Mud flakes off all over the carpet. I go across to our bathroom and run a huge steaming bath until it almost slops over the top. I pour in some green stuff of Nick's which is supposed to be good for after exercise, and it makes the bathroom smell like a forest. Nick will go mad, but who cares? I'll think about that later.

*Sarah Louise ate the apple. Why? How? How did the apple get across to Sarah Louise's time?*

I think it's something to do with the orchard.

Then.

Now.

THEN meeting NOW.

Is it me going back, or Sarah Louise coming forward? Time running backwards, and time running forwards, so that Sarah Louise meets me in the middle?

No. That makes it sound too easy. It doesn't work like that.

The car reversing down the lane. The crows rising up in a cloud. They didn't have cars in Sarah Louise's time, did they? But they had apples. Do apple trees live for a hundred years? Or maybe this tree grew from the pip of a tree which was alive in Sarah Louise's time—or from the pip of a tree which was the pip of a tree?

There has to be a connection. Something to make the link. Something between me and Sarah Louise. So what is it? Why do I feel as if Sarah Louise is inside me, right inside my thoughts?

The bath is a good place for thinking in. I turn on the hot tap with my toes, which isn't as easy as it sounds, and let out a bit of the cooling water so the bath won't overflow.

Something is happening in the orchard. Now. I don't know what it is. But I *could* know, if I wanted to. People don't wrap up packets as carefully as that, and then hide them away, all for no reason. There must be something valuable in the packet. Worth a lot of money. Tonight, I'll talk to Shell. See what she thinks. I feel better now that Shell knows, now that I'm not so much on my own any more. Shell's bright, when she's not pretending to be a little girl who hasn't noticed anything. At least she's not pretending with me any more. She feels like my sister again.

But I want to think about time. My time and Sarah Louise's time. REVERSING. The word has got a clue in it somewhere. The car reversing. Sarah Louise making my watch go back to 1892. *Time reversing?* Is that it? Am I like a car going backwards, fast, not knowing where I'm going until I smash into Sarah Louise?

Or perhaps time is different in this house. In other places time goes away once it's happened. You only get today, not yesterday and the day before and last year all happening at once.

But in this house, bits of time seem to be trapped, like old films which have never stopped running, over and over, even when there's nobody to watch them. Even though nobody wants to watch them.

Do I want to watch them? I don't know. I don't even understand the pictures I'm seeing. They are like those puzzle pictures where you have to look and find something hidden in it. Look one way, and it's just a blank, safe pattern. Look another way, and it's a house. Or a girl looking at you. Or a gun. And once you've seen the house, or the girl, or the gun, you can't go back to not seeing it. Your eyes keep on picking up the outline, even when you'd much rather not find it any more. Just as I can't go back to not knowing that Sarah Louise is there, and that I've got to help her, even though I don't know how to.

There's a pattern here, in this house, and I'm not picking it up. I'm seeing patterns, but I know there are pictures. Not just things happening *THEN*. Things happening *NOW*. Somewhere, they all join up.

Has Sarah Louise been here for a hundred years, huddled up under the house? Or has she come because we're here? Because I'm here to see her?

Perhaps other people have seen Sarah Louise. I can't be the only one. If Shell could see her, then I'd know she was real. I'd know she wasn't just inside my mind.

If only I could ask someone. Oh, Dad. I can't ask you things any more. Dad's face. *Business.*

*" . . . disappear for a bit, that's all . . . "*

*"You wouldn't believe the questions people are asking."*

But I'm not asking any questions, am I? I've been sensible, Dad. Ask no questions and you'll get told no lies. Don't ask where things come from.

Imagine if I'd said to Dad on the stairs: *"Who were those men in the orchard, Dad? What were they doing?"*

*"You're asking questions, Paulie. That's not very sensible."*

*"Dad, tell me about your business. What is it?"*

Dad's face, not funny and whistling any more, but hard and desperate. Dad hugging me, too tight. He doesn't want me to know. It's not safe for me to know.

It wouldn't work. I could never ask him that. There's got to be another way.

Once, when Shell was about seven, I got fed up with her pretending she didn't know about Father Christmas. "Oh Mum, d'you think Father Christmas could afford a TV for my room?" (This was before we were in the money.) And I was imitating her and saying, "Oh Mum, d'you think Father Christmas could get me a miniature Rolls Royce?" and that sort of stuff. Later on Mum got me on my own in the kitchen and said, "You're not to spoil it for Shell. No-one spoiled it for you." "But Mum, she *knows* it's not true. She's just putting you on so you think she's sweet and she gets more stuff."

Mum laughed. "Yes, I know she knows, I'm not stupid, but if she doesn't want to let on that she knows, then what does it matter? Sometimes people know things really, but they don't even let *themselves* know that they know them."

I didn't see Mum's point then, but I do now. Sometimes people know things really, but they don't even let *themselves* know that they know them.

*"Everybody's wondering where all the money's coming from."*

Was it Nick who said that? Or was it me? I think of the little packets. Light, and valuable. And no-one's supposed to know they're here.

It's still quiet by the time I've finished my bath and got dressed again. I'm starving. I've got a stash of Mars Bars in my room, and I eat two. I remember I haven't had any breakfast, or any dinner either. What's going on? Someone ought to be fetching Shell by now. Where's Mum?

Their bedroom door is open a bit, but there's no-one in the room. The bed's messy and some of Mum's clothes are on the floor. Thin, cold wind blows through the window and the curtain flaps out as I open the door wide. I don't usually come in here. It feels more private than their bedroom did in our old house.

I move very quietly across the room. Dad has got a little room joined on to it, which is called a dressing-room. It has a huge wardrobe made of dark wood, with carved patterns on the front, which was in the house already when we moved here. And there's a little couch you can sleep on, only Dad never does.

But he must have done last night, because the couch is all messy and tumbled too, and there's a duvet trailing on the floor. The two mirrored doors of the wardrobe are open. I push one slightly and it swings. Dad's drawers are open too, and some of his socks and pants have dropped on the floor. The hangers are bunched together as if he's been shoving them aside, looking for something. I breathe in the smell of the dressing-room: wood and leather, and some cologne for men which Mum bought Dad. He never uses it, but the bottle's open on his chest.

The dressing-room looks as if Dad's just rushed out, tying his tie as he runs downstairs, shouting goodbye to me and Mum and Shell. And at the same time it looks as empty as if Dad's been gone for a hundred years. It must be like this when people die, and you still have their things everywhere.

I back out of the dressing-room and go to Mum and Dad's window. It's grey outside, and very clear, as if it's just about to rain. Their bedroom looks down over the terrace and the long sweep of the garden away down to the woods on the left and right, and the field ahead, where the horses are. I can't see anyone working down by the silver birches. Perhaps they've knocked off already. No. There they are, coming out of the woods at the side, by the big clumps of rhododendron bushes. Three of them.

But they don't come out. They edge their way round the bushes then melt back, so for a second I can still see them against the dark rhododendrons, and then I can't and I blink and there's nothing there at all. The garden is perfectly still again. You couldn't tell there was anybody there at all.

I want to think they were the builders. Perhaps if I try, I'll believe it. Perhaps the one in the middle was Pete, only it's hard to recognise people at this distance. No. I know it wasn't Pete. Pete doesn't move like that, slow and careful but absolutely sure. I think of the packets in the orchard, and what Mum said to Dad:

111

"Don't mess with them, Micky. They can be dangerous."

I am hanging on to the curtain cord in the way Mum's always telling us not to. Suddenly I remember the open door behind me, and the light coming through it, showing up my outline in the window frame. I move sideways, not too fast, and keep to the wall as I go out of Mum and Dad's room and shut the door. And downstairs, quickly and lightly, across the hall to the kitchen, across to the invention room.

And there's Mum, sitting at the old, marked table. Her arms are folded and she's leaning forward, resting her head on them. There's a full cup of coffee in front of her, with skin on it. She looks as if she's been sitting there for ever.

"Mum?"

She turns round slowly and tiredly. Her hair is all combed straight back and tied up on the top of her head. Her eyes look small, because she isn't wearing any make-up. She frowns and looks at me carefully, a bit like she does when one of us is starting to get ill.

"You had a sleep then," she says. "That's good."

"What about Nick? Why didn't you wake me up?"

"I told him to take the day off," said Mum. "And Mrs Hannibal. I need a bit of peace and quiet. I can't hear myself think with all these people in the house."

Mum doesn't sound like she usually does when she's talking to me or Shell. She sounds tired and angry and cold, as if she's talking to a stranger. Or like she sounded last night when she was talking to Dad.

"Mum! What about Shell? She'll be waiting for you. It's quarter-to-five!"

Mum rubs her eyes with the back of her hands. "That's OK. Shell's stopping with friends for a few days, just till we get things sorted out."

"What—with Corinna?"

It's the only name I can think of, from Shell's new school.

Mum laughs as if I've said something really funny. For a minute her face looks normal again. "You must be joking! You think I'd ask them? No, she's gone back to London. She's staying with the Delaneys."

"Was she all right—I mean, didn't she mind?"

"Oh, you know Shell. She'll be fine."

"Did Dad take her?"

The cold look comes back on Mum's face. "No. Kevin Delaney came down to fetch her while you were asleep."

"I could've gone too," I say, thinking aloud. Yeah! I could have gone to the ice rink in the morning with Tony and John-Jo. We could've had lunch in McDonalds afterwards ... No more Nick. No more shadows and secrets and strangers. No more Sarah Louise.

"Well, you didn't," says Mum sharply, "so it's just you and me for now. Think you can cope with that?"

Shell's gone. Just when I was thinking I'd got her to talk to again. Just when I need her. She knows about the packets. No-one else does. And now there's only me and I'll have to decide what to do all on my own. She was starting to talk and share things with me again. Why've they sent her away? Do they know she knows? No, they can't.

Unless. Unless she said something. While I was asleep.

"Did she say anything, Mum? I mean, leave a message for me, or something?"

"She wanted you to go with her. But your dad thinks it's better if we go tomorrow."

"What're we going to do, Mum?"

I didn't mean to say it like that. The way it comes out, it sounds desperate. It sounds the way criminals talk in films when they've got people closing in on them from all sides. It sounds the way Dad looked on the stairs.

Mum doesn't tell me not to be so stupid. She gives me a quick, close look and says quietly. "Better if you just carry on the way you normally do, Paul. You know. Go down and see the horses, have a chat with Pete. Nick'll be here tomorrow to do your lessons with you. Don't say anything to him. Then we'll go off in the evening. Just for a while, till things quieten down. It's all been a bit hectic lately."

She's trying to sound calm and cheerful now. But I've got to tell her.

"Mum. I don't think we ought to go down the garden." I'm whispering. I don't know why.

Mum looks up at me. Her eyes have gone large again, and very dark. "Why, Paulie? What's the matter?"

"There's three men down there. I saw them."

Mum jolts in the chair and then grabs my hand tight and pulls me close to her. "Where did you see them?"

"Down the bottom of the garden, by the woods, coming out of the bushes. Then they went back in."

"My God," says Mum softly. Her fingers are hurting mine, but I don't want to say anything. "Paulie. Did you see them? Did you see what they looked like?"

"I couldn't really. They were too far away."

"Listen. This might sound a bit of a funny question. But it's important. Have you ever seen any of them before? Have any of them ever come to the house? On business?"

I try to think back. The way they moved, the way they melted into the bushes. No. I can't tell. "They might've. I don't know. But why would they hide, if they come here, anyway?"

Mum looks down at the table. She says very quietly,

"No, they wouldn't come themselves. They'd send people . . . " and the way she says it makes the skin crawl on my arms. Then Mum seems to realise I'm still there. "Right. Paulie. It's all right. *Nothing to worry about.* Only I'll have to make a phone call. No. Wait a minute. Get me a bit of paper."

There's a memo pad in the kitchen, but no pen. Dad's always swearing about that, when we take the pen for something else. Now I swear too, because it's not there when I need it. I find a stump of pencil on the fridge and skid back across the floor to Mum.

She scribbles down a number. I can tell by the code it's a central London one.

"It's best if *you* talk, Paul, just in case. Let it ring five times. If no-one answers, hang up. When they pick up the phone, they won't say anything. You just say, *'We think Uncle Bill might be coming for Christmas after all.'* They won't answer. When you hear them put the phone down, come straight back here."

The nearest phone is in the kitchen, on the wall. A bright scarlet phone. Mum chose the colour. I pick it up and start to dial the number, then I stop. There's no sound at all coming out of the phone. I give it a shake and dial anyway, but nothing happens.

"Mum!" I call. "There's something wrong with the phone!"

In a second she's beside me. "Don't shout!" she says. She holds the receiver up to her ear and listens, then drops it on the kitchen counter. "OK. Never mind, we can still—Oh God. Your dad's got the carphone." Mum bangs her fist on the counter. The phone jumps.

Outside, it's getting dusky. It seems to get dark earlier in the country. And there are no street-lights.

Mum crosses to the window and pulls down the blinds. Then she comes back and switches on the lights. "No point in advertising where we are," she says.

"Mum, turn the lights off!"

Mum sighs as if she's very tired. "They know we're here, Paulie."

"Mum. *Who are they?*"

"It'll be all right Paulie. *Don't get frightened*. It's to do with your dad's business. There's a few things gone wrong, and he's trying to sort it out. He's doing his best. But some of the people he's in business with don't understand. They get impatient. We just have to be careful—"

She breaks off. There's a sound outside the kitchen window. Just a slight sound. One of those little country sounds that frighten you at first before you get used to them.

Now all my skin prickles and goes tight.

"Mum!"

Mum's face suddenly goes terrible. She backs up against the counter and her hand reaches out, reaches behind her, feeling for something on the wall. Where we hang the knives. The new set of sharp knives Dad bought. They cut through every sort of meat, just like cutting through cheese.

"Mum, don't!"

"Quick, Paulie! It's all right. They're not going to hurt us. Go on upstairs. Get in your room and lock the door and whatever happens, whatever you hear, *don't come out*. Get right in the back of your wardrobe and pull the clothes in front of you. They'll think you've gone with Shell. *Whatever happens*, stay in there."

"Mum, I can't, I can't! You've got to come!"

And I'm hanging on to her and trying to drag her through the kitchen door but she's still a bit stronger than me and she unpeels my hands and shoves me away from her and she hisses in a voice I've never heard before, "Go NOW. GO, Paulie!"

And I look at her face and go.

# Chapter Thirteen

Skid over the floor. Bang against the heavy door into the hall. My shoulder! A jolt of pain like electricity going up my neck. Don't stop. The big dark hall. The dark well of the stairs like an open mouth.

No! Twist, turn, scutter back. The kitchen. Lights. *MUM* . . .

*Doan 'it me. Doan 'ert me.*

*Don't hit me. Don't hurt me.*

I never went back. I just left her there. Sarah Louise! Mum!

Mum can't hear me. She's listening to something else. I freeze in the kitchen doorway, watching her. I want to run to her and hide, like I did when I was a little kid and Mum could make everything better, but I can't. My legs won't take me. She's standing with her back to me, just to one side of the back door, listening, listening. Her right hand is down by her side, clenched. She's holding something and I know what it is. And I'm frightened. I'm in a nightmare where I can't speak to her or reach her. I'm afraid that if she turns round, it won't be Mum's face any more. It'll be another mask, even more terrible than the one on Dad's face.

Everything's still except for an electric humming

noise from the fluorescent lights. It's the stillness you get just after a flash of lightning, while the thunder gathers itself to crack out overhead. I creep back from the doorway. Mum doesn't move. She hasn't seen me. She's like a weapon by the back door, listening. I listen too.

I can't hear anything. Only a hum like news travelling down the telegraph wires along the lane to Cold Haven. You hear the hum, but you don't hear the words. The phone's gone dead. They've cut the line. I can't hear anything.

But I can.

*Paul. Paul.*

Not a cry. Not a shout. A whisper that runs through me, into my bones. It's Sarah Louise. Sarah Louise, alone and terrified. And she's calling me.

*Paul. Paul.*

Each time she says my name the sound is thinner and more desperate. As if she's calling me with her last breath. I move through the scullery. Her voice pulls me away from Mum, away from the kitchen, away from NOW. I go through the cellar door, down the steps, across the furnace-room. I pick up the torch.

It's never been so easy to get into the passage. My shoulder burns but I fit into the space as smoothly as a plug into its socket. The voice comes again, more strongly, PAUL, PAUL!. I haul myself along towards it as if I'm being pulled to safety along the rope of the voice. The dry dust makes me cough but there's a wind blowing along, a warm wind from a furnace which was lit a hundred years ago.

And round the corner Sarah Louise crawls to meet me.

Her shawl has come off and her raggy hair hangs round her shoulders. But she's looking at me, looking out for me, and I've never seen anything like her face.

She's alive. More alive than anyone I've ever seen. How could I have thought she was a ghost? Ghosts don't look like this.

Once I saw a rocket go off over the Thames. It climbed up so high we thought it wasn't going to explode at all, then it came down in gold fountains from the top of the sky to the edge of Southwark and I saw Mum's and Shell's faces all golden from it. Sarah Louise looks like that, only the fountain is inside her. It's not a reflection.

And she's been looking for me. That's why she's so joyful, because I've come at last. She grabs my arm and her sharp fingers pinch me hard.

"I bin so worried. I thought Mrs Cann'nball'd got yer fer sure! I bin waitin' and waitin' fer yer! Lissen! Carn yer 'ear it? 'Ear 'ow quiet it is? They've gorn! They've all gorn! We kin get away, up through th' Orchid. Now's the chance!"

I listen. No sound but the heat sighing down the passageway. No sound but the dull distant roar of the furnace.

"But what about the furnace?" I say.

"They've gorn, I'm tellin yer! Gorn ter beggary! We kin get out through the gratins, same's I got in. They've gorn. Mrs Cann'nball. Mr Mord'n. Mrs Perfeck. Th'ole boilin'.'"

"But how do you know they've gone?" I ask, staring at her. Her hand is burning hot where she's holding on to my arm.

"I seen em! I seen em all, goin' across th'Orchid. Three of em, all in a row. One, two three. Pretty maids."

She laughs loudly, stumbling against me. How thin and light she is. Burning up, like a handful of dry sticks thrown on a bonfire. How long is it since she had anything to eat?

"But what about the Admiral? He'll still be here."

"'E's not in th'kitchin. 'E's up above. 'E won't 'ear us goin'.'"

Then a thought strikes me.

"Sarah Louise. Sarah Louise. How *could* you see them, when you're stuck down here?"

She frowns and shakes her head as if it hurts. Then she smiles and I see her awful teeth. They're crumbly and she's got some missing. "I seen em clear as I see yer face now, I swear t'God. Goin' on their evil ways smilin'. They've gorn!"

Perhaps she's got a fever. When people have got a fever they see things that aren't real. But maybe . . . maybe Sarah Louise really *can* see things other people can't see. After all she's not like other people.

"But they'll come back! They might be on their way back now."

Then I think of the three men coming out of the bushes. Maybe that was what Sarah Louise saw? But how could she? How could she look out from one century to another as if she was looking through a window? Just as I looked out of Mum and Dad's window and saw the men coming?

Sarah Louise thinks she is safe. She thinks she can come up through the central heating gratings into the house to escape and she won't be caught. I shiver, thinking of Mrs Cann'nball waiting like a cat by a mousehole. Down here, Mrs Cann'nball seems more real than the three men, more real than the little sound outside the kitchen, more real even than Mum. Mrs Cann'nball with her smooth savage face, her arms like bars, beating Sarah Louise. Mrs Cann'nball waiting for Sarah Louise, because Sarah Louise knows something she shouldn't know. Something dangerous.

*Just like me.* I know things I shouldn't know. I'm hiding too. Maybe that's it. That's the link between me and Sarah Louise. I've found the connection. That's why she can make me see things. That's why I can see her.

My heart bumps with excitement. It's all coming clear! I grab Sarah Louise, to tell her. No. It's too complicated. There's no time. We've got to escape.

Mum is vague and far away. I can't think about her properly. When I try to get a picture of Mum's face in my mind, it slips out of focus like a little ball of mercury running away from your fingers.

"Yeah," says Sarah Louise. "They'll be back. So we got ter go NOW."

And she pinches me harder, and grins as if she's really just a kid, not Sarah Louise at all. Her face is bony, like the bird's skull I found in the woods. It must have been there a long time because the bones were picked clean, greyish-white. Birds must be dying all the time, but you don't see them much. You'd think London streets would be covered in dead sparrows and pigeons, but they aren't. The birds must use their last bit of strength to go away and hide in dark, quiet places, and then they die.

"Gawd, yer slow, aren't yer?" says Sarah Louise, but she says it in a friendly way. Then she gives me a little push.

I'm moving before I've decided what to do. Sarah Louise decides for both of us. I find I'm shuffling backwards, almost as if Sarah Louise is pushing me, the way she was pulling me towards her down the passage. The warm wind is on my back. Suddenly I feel as if a light is coming on inside me, too. It's going to be all right. It's all right once you're not alone any more. First of all Shell, now Sarah Louise. We're going to get away. All of us.

# Chapter Fourteen

I feel my way backwards, bumping and scraping. If I could turn round, I could use the torch to see where I'm going, but I can't turn round. It's too narrow and I'm afraid of getting stuck if I try. Stuck down here, like Sarah Louise. The wind on my back isn't warm any more. It's hot and smoky and it makes my eyes sting. It's like the hot breath of something alive. I'm starting to prickle with sweat down the middle of my back. Sarah Louise catches hold of my hurt shoulder.

"Yer doan go back that way! Yer'll end up in th'furniss!"

She scrabbles on her knees, feeling down the bricks on the side wall. She's so skinny that she manages to eel her way past me, pressing me right up against the wall. It's rough and warm. It smells of something familiar but I can't remember what it is. It's not the same as the kiln smell. The smell niggles like a fly buzzing round my face. I know! It's the smell of the inside of the Aga, when it's lit. The smell of the inside of the slow oven when Mrs Hannibal puts a stew in it. We must be near the furnace. Perhaps it's just here, just the other side of a few bricks, roaring with flames. In a minute I'll see fire through the cracks in the bricks. A fire that was lit a hundred years ago. Will it burn me? There's a smell of burning coke and the walls are black with soot which is coming off all over us. The torch is getting dim and I shake it. The bulb brightens and then goes dull yellow again.

"'Ere y'are!" says Sarah Louise triumphantly, and she disappears, wriggling through a hole in the side of the passage. It's even narrower than the space I'm in now. I'm not sure I can get through. I'll have to put my torch in my mouth like explorers do. But it's too big and it has a horrible rubber taste. I haul myself round a bit sideways, barking my skin on the rough bricks and getting soot in my mouth. I spit it out. I follow Sarah Louise's feet. The passage isn't so narrow after all. And it's not so hot here. Sarah Louise is crawling quite fast and she manages to get her head round and hiss to me, "We got ter climb 'ere."

Of course. We're still down at cellar level. We've got to get up into the house. There'll be steps.

But there aren't steps. The passage just stops. Then it goes up, vertical, like a chimney. I screw my head round by Sarah Louise's feet and peer up. Greyish light again. More brick. A round high flue. Going somewhere? It must be, or there wouldn't be any light.

Sarah Louise straightens. "Get back!" she whispers. "I carn stand with yer 'ead in the way."

There's no room for me. I shuffle myself back, into the dark. I hate the feeling of not being able to turn round. I keep thinking someone's going to grab my legs. No. Mustn't think of it.

"Mind yer 'ead!" says Sarah Louise. "I'm goin' up."

Going up? How can she? But she does. There's a flurry of shawl and skirts and she's gone. I shuffle forward and see her going up the flue, arms and legs braced against the brick walls. Like a chimney sweep boy. Up and up. She blocks the light with her skirts.

The flue's narrow. Maybe it won't be so hard after all. If Sarah Louise can manage it . . .

And suddenly she's gone. There's just an empty circle of grey. And her voice. "I'm waitin' fer yer!"

She must've gone into a hole leading off the flue. She hasn't climbed all the way up. She must have reached the kitchen level.

Slowly I pull myself upright. My back hurts. My shoulder! I'm not going to be able to do it. I brace my hands against the rough walls. There are plenty of grips. Corners of bricks stick out for holds. But first I have to hoist myself up. It's like a fire in my shoulder when I try. A little noise comes out of my mouth. I didn't mean it to.

I flop back. I can't. Wait a minute, I'll just get my breath.

Sarah Louise's voice floats down the shaft. "Paul! Paul! I'm up 'ere! I'm waitin' fer yer! Doan worry!"

Fancy Sarah Louise telling me not to worry. She's got enough to worry about herself. I nearly laugh in the darkness.

Got to try again. Pain. Doesn't matter. It won't kill you. It's only your shoulder. No, I can't, I can't. There's a funny taste in my mouth.

"Paul! Paul! I'm 'ere!"

Just this foot. Fit it in. OK. Now the other. Waving in space, finding nothing. Now a rasp of brick. A toe-hold. Got it. Now up again. Pull with my other arm. Now the right foot. Got it. Now the shoulder. Got to. Burning hot. Furnace. And over to my left foot. I can do it. Again. Again.

And she's there. Her bare foot. Her face turned round, waiting for me. A white glimmer, that's all, and then she shuffles forward into the passage so there's room for me to climb in after her.

I can't move any more. I lie there, trying not to

be sick. It's the Mars bars, that's all, and not eating anything all day. Sarah Louise is crawling away, thinking I'm following. She's going to leave me on my own.

"Wait," I try to say, but my voice doesn't come out. *Wait, wait*, I say in my mind.

I hear her stop moving. Her voice again. "Are yer comin'? Are yer all right?"

"No," I croak out. "Give me a minute."

"There's no 'urry," says Sarah Louise. She shuffles backwards to me. I feel her hand patting my shoulder, trying to find my face. Her hand is light and hot.

"It's my shoulder," I say, "I hurt it."

"No 'urry," says Sarah Louise again.

But I know we've got to hurry. How long have we been down here?

"Th'gratin's just along 'ere. See where the light's coming from? The gratin comes out in Mrs Cann'nball's kitchin."

This must be one of the ventilation shafts for the old boiler system – unless it's another heating duct? But they wouldn't need heating in the kitchen, would they? So does the passage come out through the floor or out of the wall? I can't remember seeing a heating duct in our kitchen, in our time.

*Maybe it's been covered over and Sarah Louise doesn't know. We'll never get out of here!*

My heart thumps against the inside of my arm. Sweat's tickling the sides of my face and I can't wipe it off, there isn't room. We're going to come out into Mrs Cannonball's kitchen. Sarah Louise says it just as if it's a normal room. But if I come out into Mrs Cannonball's kitchen, I'll be coming out into the past. You can't tell if these passages are in the past or in the present. They look just the same. That's why I still don't know if I'm in Sarah Louise's time, or if she's in mine. But I think I must be in Sarah Louise's time now, or else why would it be so hot? In my time, the furnace hasn't been lit for years.

I'm going to come out of the passage into a hundred years ago.

## Chapter Fifteen

But we are here, now. I can feel the heat of Sarah Louise's body. She's as alive as I am. If I'm not a ghost of the future, she isn't a ghost of the past. I can go on now.

I press Sarah Louise's arm to show her I'm ready to go. She pulls her shawl round her again, to protect her elbows from the brickwork, and eases her way forward. A few feet farther on, she stops. I can't see past her, to find out why she's stopped. But I can see light coming round her, outlining her body. Sharp, real light. Not the faint grey light that seeps through these shafts and passageways. Not torchlight either. But it doesn't look like daylight. She's right. We're coming out into the heart of the house. Into the kitchen.

"S'all right!" whispers Sarah Louise. She wriggles and one of her hard bare feet kicks me in the mouth. It hurts and I make a noise and she kicks again, gently, to shut me up. Her bare feet are just as hard as feet with shoes on.

"Gratin's loose," she whispers, "I got ter feel fer it."

She rolls on her side and now I can see the square mesh of the grating in front of us, with cut-up squares of light shining through it. She's feeling at the sides, scrabbling all the way round. Her fingers look black against the light, working away. Very slow, very careful. Only a little plastery noise. Nobody could hear it. Or if they did, they might think it was just a mouse.

Then Sarah Louise gives the grating a little hitch in a special place in one corner. She must have fixed it like this, balanced but not really closed, after she climbed in. How long ago? How does she feel, going back where she said she'd never go? The grating slips but there's no other metal for it to clang against so it still doesn't make much noise. A thud against the wall. It hangs sideways, and the opening is wide enough for Sarah Louise to slip through.

But she doesn't. She curls her body round and feels for my hand. It trembles in mine, and now I know how frightened she is. She hasn't shown it before. She's waited for me, listened out for me, told me where to go. But now she doesn't want to be alone, going out through that grating.

We can't go together. There's only just enough space for one at a time, or else we'll both get stuck.

Sarah Louise looks at me as if she wants to tell me something, but she doesn't open her mouth. I look at her eyes. They are shining. Is it because she's ill? Is it because . . .

I look into Sarah Louise's eyes and I see a girl curled up asleep on a pile of rags in the corner of a scullery. She has a blanket but it's thin and it doesn't cover her properly. She twitches it and pulls it tight to try and keep warm. The floor of the scullery is cold stone, and there's a tap dripping. Next door is the warm kitchen, where they keep a fire going in the range all night, but she's not allowed to sleep there. And she's not allowed to sleep on a truckle bed in the attics with Becky and Nell and Sarah Partridge and all the other girls. She's done wrong. They're punishing her. They don't want Sarah Louise blabbing to the girls about what she's seen. About what she knows.

I look into Sarah Louise's eyes and I see the girl wake up with a jerk as she hears the first clatter from the kitchen. She stumbles off her bed and rubs her hands over her face. No time to wash. She kicks the rags into the corner and pushes back her hair. There's coal to be fetched for the range. The range is hungry, eating coal all day and all night. It must be fed. She daren't think what would happen to her if she let the range go out.

The buckets of coal are too heavy for her. It should be one of the lads doing the job, but Mrs Cann'nball has told them to leave the job to Sarah Louise, "*Let 'er do it. She's little enough use in my kitchen. And I carn 'ave 'er going upstairs looking like that. Look at the dirt on 'er.*"

Sarah Louise doesn't want to be dirty. She'd like to wash off the coal and grease, but there's no time, no hot water. And she's not allowed to wash herself under the pump in the yard, as the men do. She catches Becky looking at her, half-frightened, half-sorry. But not daring to say anything. Not daring to do anything, for fear it'll be her turn next.

It's all right at night. She dreams, just like everyone else, not like a slavey. She dreams of fields and sun and flowers. She dreams of the orchard. She wakes up to coal buckets and pails of scrubbing water, and the smell of her rags. She staggers out into the grey yard to get the coal.

Later they start the cooking. The smell of meat roasting on the range is like two hands squeezing in the sides of her stomach. She holds her hand over her mouth.

The flames leap up in the range, then die down to a hot red glow. Mrs Cann'nball kneels to test the heat of the slow oven. "Perfect," she says, and there stands Mrs Perfeck, the housekeeper, in her crackling apron, not too near the fire for fear of the spit of meat-juices.

"'Ow's that girl of yours getting on?" she asks.

"I'm keepin' my eye on 'er," says Mrs Cann'nball.

"You do that," says Mrs Perfeck.

They look at one another and they nod. Fat spurts out of the side of beef and flares, then is swallowed up by the flames.

Sarah Louise ghosts past with the big dripping-pan which she's got to scrub. It is black and burning hot. Everyone moves aside to make way for her, but no-one looks at her face. It's as if they are all afraid to look at her. The lads who used to pass a word with her when they came in with the coal. Sarah Partridge who embroidered a handkerchief for her last Christmas. Becky who used to help Sarah Louise plait up her hair at night, when they were dog-tired but still giggling up in the attic. None of them talk to her now. Bad luck sits on her like a spell. And Mrs Cann'nball watching. You can't get past Mrs Cann'nball. And life's hard enough for all of them, never mind helping Sarah Louise.

The pictures fade. I blink, and shiver. I've seen more than I wanted to see. Sarah Louise is still looking at me, but there are no more pictures. I've seen enough.

She smiles, and puts her finger on her lips. "Time ter go," she whispers. "Mind yer 'ead when yer go. There's a bit of a drop down. I'll be waitin' fer yer."

Sarah Louise crouches right by the grating. She hunches her back, wriggles up her knees till they are tucked right under her, and grasps the opening at each side with her hands. The light vanishes. She fills the gap for a few seconds, bracing herself, then she grunts and dives forward. One of her feet catches on the grating. She falls awkwardly, caught by the foot. There's a dull thump, then her foot flips free. Then nothing. I've shut my eyes.

I don't open them. I can't. I don't want to see any more pictures. I don't want to watch THEN turn into NOW. I'll only get out of here if I hold my breath and keep my eyes shut. I feel for the sides of the grating. I crouch like Sarah Louise. Don't look down. Put your head between your knees.

*Don't look down! Dive, Paulie, dive!*

Dad's voice. Dad's voice from long ago, at the swimming-baths at home.

And I make my dive, the kind of bad dive you do at swimming-baths just when all your friends have turned to watch. And then you come up through thick chlorinated water with your eyes stinging and a red slap on your chest, and you see a little round circle of light up above you getting bigger and bigger and then you burst through it. There's a roar of noise and for a second everything's strange and a bit frightening after the silence underwater. You flick your head to get rid of the wet hair in your face and shout to your friends and it's all back to normal.

But not here. I'm underwater, and I'm on dry land, both at once. Sarah Louise breaks my fall. I can't move. I lie there with that sick awful feeling you have after a dream of falling, when you jolt awake in your bed. Sarah Louise lies sprawled out, and my face is in her hair. I'm so close I'm looking right into her hair. There's things crawling in it, loads of them. Lice. They wouldn't let her keep herself clean.

I push myself up a bit, away from her. We haven't fallen far, I'm sure we haven't. But she's quite still. She's got her head twisted round as if she's still trying to look behind her, to see if I'm coming. The tiles on the floor are hard and cold. There's a bit of blood. It can't be a bad cut. There'd be more blood. It can't be serious. It's coming out of her ear. *Out of her ear*. A flash of my school First Aid course comes back to me. Mrs Winter.

*"If there has been a blow to the head, or a fall, there may be bleeding from the nose or the ears. DON'T TOUCH THE INJURED PERSON. IT MAY BE SERIOUS. Go for help. You can do more damage by rushing in thinking you know everything—yes, Paul, I am looking at you—"*

A little creeping thread of blood on the hard, shiny, dark-red tiles. *Go for help*. But there's nowhere to go now. Sarah Louise has got no-one but me. I've never seen these tiles before. And something's gone quiet. Something inside me isn't there any more. A voice has gone quiet. Her voice.

I look up. A broad band of thick, black, dull-shining metal. Bars. A big red fire sucks and roars. It's behind bars. There's a heat shimmer over it like you get on hot roads in summer. I know it's the range, because I've seen it before.

Not a shimmer. A curtain of fire. Behind it there's something else. Figures forming like shapes made out of heat.

A tall man in black with white hands hanging by his sides. Mr Mord'n.

A round, rosy woman in a white apron with a big bunch of keys around her waist. You wouldn't think she was frightening until you looked at her face. But I know her. Mrs Perfeck.

A broad woman in black. Her arms are thick all the way down, like boards. Her flesh looks hard as wood. Her hands are raw red. She's got a bit of dark greasy hair screwed up on the top of her head, so tight it pulls her eyes up at the corners. Her. *The Holy Queen of Heav'n*. Her. *Mrs Kick-yer-arse-Cann'nball*.

Not a shimmer. A curtain. A fourth figure, a man wearing clothes like the ones I've seen on TV serials about rich people in the olden days. The kind of serial Mum always switches off. White waistcoat. Big gold watch. Lots of hair growing down the sides of his face. But look again. Look at his face. He reminds me of someone I know. Who is it? He's like—

A shiver of ice runs all over me.

"DAD!" I scream.

Sarah Louise doesn't stir. The Admiral smiles.

"Dad," I say again, this time so quietly only Sarah Louise could hear me. But Sarah Louise doesn't hear me.

Nick's voice in my head: *"He came into a pile of money from somewhere. Nobody really knows anything about it. And he built this place out of it."*

"Just like Dad," I whisper.

Nick's voice again, *"You wouldn't believe the questions people are asking."*

Questions about Dad. *"Where does the money come from? What does he do for a living? Funny sort of business, it must be."*

Who said that? Mrs Hannibal? Mrs Cann'nball? WHO'S SPEAKING?

The Admiral smiles through the curtain of heat which is parting all the time as the four figures grow clearer and closer. Mrs Cann'nball. Mr Mord'n. Mrs Perfeck. Th'Amiral.

*"Why is she weepin'*
*weepin' weepin'"*

Sarah Louise's thin little singing voice is in my head again. She has only got me now. She has looked after me, and now I've got to look after her, no matter what happens. Mr Mord'n. Mrs Perfeck. Mrs Cann'nball. The Admiral.

Oh, Sarah Louise. I can see why you were so frightened now. And I can see why you were so frightened then. Time's joining up. I can see why you stayed frightened for a hundred years. They would never let you rest.

They don't say anything. I am backing away from them, up against Sarah Louise. She hasn't opened her eyes. I'm glad that she can't see them. I'm glad she doesn't know what's happening. She doesn't know that it's all gone wrong. She hasn't escaped after all. They're here to get her. THEN has become NOW.

I grab hold of Sarah Louise and pull her towards me. She doesn't weigh much but she's hard to hold. Her head flops forward onto my shoulder and her hair gets into my mouth. I am right up against the kitchen wall now and they're still coming, strolling through the air as if they're out for a walk on a summer's day, as if they don't mean any harm to anyone. I look behind me but there aren't any knives hanging on the wall.

I grip Sarah Louise tight. There isn't anywhere to go now. The Admiral looks at me, and holds out his arms. He holds out his arms like someone who never doubts for a minute that he's going to get what he wants. He always has. And Mrs Cann'nball waits with her arms folded. It will be her turn next. They know I'm going to do what they want. Everybody always does.

And I nearly give way and let them take her. But just at that moment I feel something go through her, not a sound or a movement but a funny little sigh, up close to my ear. I think I feel her escaping breath.

"You're not having her!" I scream. "She got away! YOU'RE NOT HAVING HER."

And as I scream at them they come closer and closer so I can see nothing except them stooping and looming, and then Mrs Cann'nball puts up her arm and . . .

. . . and like a photograph you hold too close they go out of focus and dazzle away into blotches of black and white and they dance for a moment then dissolve.

I clutch Sarah Louise tight. I have got her, and they are gone. She sighs again, and there's a last, light puff of breath, like someone saying goodbye. I hold her tight, even though she's safe now. And then her frame of bones melts between my hands. I clutch. I think I feel a trace of her warmth. But she is gone.

I look up. The curtain of heat from the range wavers and disappears. The harsh dark-red tiles soften, and turn blue-and-white, and the kitchen is full of fluorescent lights, people and voices, and a tall black figure stoops down to me. A man in uniform.

And there is Mum at the table with the three men sitting around her. Her head is down, resting on her elbows. She doesn't look at me.

"No damage," says the uniformed policeman. "The lad fainted, that's all."

"Not surprising with all that's been going on round here," says the policewoman who has just bent down to put a cup of tea in front of Mum. Steam curls out of it, away up to the ceiling.

"I don't know where he is. I don't know what you're doing here," says Mum, in the kind of voice that sounds as if she's said it already, over and over again.

My hands are still clenched tight over nothing. "Sarah Louise," I say. I only say it to myself but one of the men at the table looks up sharply.

"Who's that?" he asks me.

"Nothing. She's gone."

The man makes a note on his pad, then nobody says anything.

She's gone, I think. I'm not sad. I thought I was, but I'm not. I'm full of happiness, that kind of happiness which is fierce, like flames. She got away. She escaped, just like she thought she was going to. All that fear is gone, a hundred years of it. She never saw Mrs Cann'nball again, or Mrs Perfeck, or Mr Mord'n, or Th'Amiral. She never even knew that they were there to get her.

*You didn't get her*, I think fiercely. *And now you'll never get her.*

## Chapter Sixteen

It was good organisation Dad, but it can't have been good enough. Now I know why you and Mum were arguing all night, the night before you left. And I know why your clothes were all over the place and your drawers were left hanging open. There wasn't much time. You knew they were after you. But who did you think was after you? Just the police, or your 'business associates' as well?

*"I still don't like it. I've got a feeling. You've been too lucky."*

*"What's luck got to do with it? It's organisation."*

*"When'll we know?"*

*"The last drop's on Friday."*

*"God, I wish it was all over."*

We were lucky it was the police, not the people Mum thought it was when I told her about the three men hiding in the bushes. I know now that it wasn't the police Mum was afraid of when she grabbed that knife and told me to hide up in the wardrobe and not come out whatever happened. There's worse than the police when you're in the money and it's come the way our money came. The way I think our money came. We don't talk about it. It's still never been said out loud.

But I know. It wasn't because of the police that they sent Shell away up to London.

And now it *is* all over, the way Mum wanted it to be. But not quite. She didn't want Dad to go. That night, did she know he was going for good? The only things I don't know now are the ones I don't want to know, ever.

I was right about Nick watching us. Mum knew, too. We never saw him again. Nick wanted the job as tutor all right, but he had more than one reason for wanting it. And we weren't the only ones paying him. But he came too late. By the time he got into Cold Haven, the game was nearly over.

All that time at Cold Haven there were people watching us. When Shell and I were down in the woods. When I was talking to Pete. Did Pete know? Did they ask him too?

*"Anything you see, anything unusual, just give us a call. We're always here."*

I don't want to think Pete knew. You have to believe that some people liked you just for yourself, and wanted to talk to you out of friendliness.

But none of those watchers got what they were looking for. Dad had gone. And of course the packets weren't there any longer either. After that there weren't any more cars backing up to the Old Orchard, up the track through the woods. No more crows rising up in the air and screaming because there were strangers moving through the trees and the long grass.

They came too late, those three men and all the men in uniforms with radios and sirens blaring down the lanes who came after them. Dad had already gone. Mum and I didn't know anything. And it didn't do them any good going to London to interview Shell. Even the police could see that a kid like Shell couldn't possibly know anything. A lovely kid like Shell.

I know it's wrong, what Dad did. Where the money came from. I knew it even before I saw the Admiral's face in that kitchen a hundred years ago, with that smile on it as if he'd seen everything and done everything. And when I saw that he looked like Dad. Or Dad looked like him. After all, the Admiral came first. He was here all the time. There was a bit of Dad's face in the Admiral's. Just a look. Something they've both got in their eyes. Then I knew what *business* had done to Dad, bit by bit, so slowly I'd never had to notice it before.

I don't know what I'd do if I saw Dad now. You never know when things are happening for the last time, like that hug he gave me on the stairs. I'm sure now that I was right when I thought he wanted to cry, too. Then I feel sorry for Dad, even though I don't want to feel sorry for him. I've got to think of us now. Mum and Shell and me. Dad turned and ran down the stairs just the way he did every morning. He didn't say goodbye. But he must have known he was going.

I don't know where Dad's gone. Maybe Mum knows, but she's not saying anything, and I haven't asked. That's not quite true. I think Mum *would* tell me, if I asked. It must be lonely for her, knowing so many things and not being able to tell anybody.

And Shell will never ask. She's back at her old school, back with her old friends. Nobody says anything about it to Shell. I know she misses Dad, but she doesn't ask any questions. I try to get her to talk to me a bit, because I don't think it's good for her to hide everything. The police have nearly stopped coming round, but they're still close. Still watching, and waiting for Dad to come out of his hole. They think in the end he'll take a risk, do something stupid. Try to see us. But I don't think he will.

We're not in the money any more. It's all gone.

Cold Haven, the car, the swimming-pool they were building. All the people who were working for us. The Hannibals wouldn't even come up to the house to get their wages. Mum had to post them. Maybe they were frightened, maybe they didn't want to have anything to do with us any more.

We've got a flat not far from our old house in London, so I'm back at my old school, with my friends. It's not quite the same though. You can call a place '*home*' in your mind, but when you come back it's changed. Or maybe I've changed. In a way I don't even want it to be the same. That would be like saying nothing had happened. We'd never been away. No Cold Haven, no Old Orchard. No Sarah Louise. I'm the only person who knows about Sarah Louise. If I don't remember her, and what happened to her, it'll be gone for ever.

Steve didn't come round much when we first moved into the flat. And he was always busy when I asked him to go out. But it's getting better, now he knows we're not in the money any more.

Mum's got a job in a travel agency. That's what we live on now. Most of the new toys and clothes and stuff have broken or worn out. Even Shell's sweaters. It's amazing how much Shell has grown. Now it doesn't seem real, that we had all those things and I could open my window and look over the terrace and the rose bushes, down the lawns which had pale shadows in the grass from flower-beds that used to be there, perhaps a hundred years ago. Down to the field with the horses nuzzling up against each other or the young ones suddenly spurting off for no reason and galloping to the other side of the field.

No Old Orchard soaked with dew at six o'clock in the morning. No stripy green-and-rust apples thumping through the long grass and splitting open by my boots. No letting my camp-fire burn down until I could push back the charred sticks and wedge apples wrapped in foil over the red core of the fire. I miss the quiet, though I never thought I would.

I've got my watch back. It was lying on the kitchen floor. It must have come off her wrist when she fell. It was too big for her anyway. I wish the watch had stayed on Sarah Louise. It only tells one time now. It won't ever tell that other time again.

I looked for Sarah Louise's gravestone in the churchyard, before we left Cold Haven. Some of the names had worn away so I couldn't read them. I ran my fingers over them, feeling for her name. But she wasn't there. They'd probably have put ANNIE on her gravestone anyway, not SARAH LOUISE. It would be cheaper.

*"They give me Annie here. Not Sarah Louise. They doan give me Sarah Louise cos it's too fancy, see."*

She wasn't supposed to have a fancy name, because she didn't deserve one. She was only a servant. A secret servant they wouldn't allow up in the house any more. A secret servant who waited under the house for a hundred years, until I came.

"Where are yer, Paul? I bin waitin'."

Sarah Louise was caught in that trap of fear for a hundred years. No-one ever came to let her out, in all that time. Mrs Cann'nball. Mrs Perfeck. Mr Mord'n. The Admiral. They put her in it. They made a trap for her like the mole-traps Mr Hannibal used to put down at Cold Haven to kill the moles that spoiled his lawns with their tunnelling. He still does, I suppose. *There have always been Hannibals at Cold Haven.* But there's no Sarah Louise at Cold Haven any more, trapped and waiting. And no Tiernans. Did I let her out? Or did she let me out? It doesn't matter. We're both free of that house now.

I looked all round the graveyard, but I didn't really think I'd find her. The graveyard was mossy, and quiet. A man was mowing the long grass down by the wall. I smelled the petrol-fumes from his mower, and he gave me a wave as he turned the machine. He didn't know who I was. That was the last time I went up to the village. I went on my own. I had a crazy feeling that I might hear her voice again. But there was only the putter of the motor-mower, so I had to be the first one to speak.

"*Sarah Louise. Sarah Louise.*"

There wasn't any answer. Wherever she is, she can't hear me calling her, like a voice down a long dark passage.

"*Sarah Louise ...*"

She isn't waiting, or listening. She doesn't need me any more.

I didn't find her grave. I expect they hid her away somewhere quickly, out of sight, not far from the house.

Also available in DEFINITIONS

*Postcards from No Man's Land* by Aidan Chambers

*I Capture the Castle* by Dodie Smith

*Going to Egypt* by Helen Dunmore

*Now I Know* by Aidan Chambers

*Amongst the Hidden* by Margaret Haddix

*The Tower Room* by Adèle Geras

*The Leap* by Jonathan Stroud

*Running out of Time* by Margaret Haddix

*Love. in Cyberia* by Chloë Rayban

*Terminal Chic* by Chloë Rayban